RESCUE!

Joe sensed rather than saw the presence of
the Germans behind him. He jerked his head
round: the first infantrymen were outlined
on the summit of the ridge, five hundred
yards away, a section of eight or more in an
irregular line. They seemed to be hesitating,
uncertain whether the lone Hurricane in the
valley might be part of an ambush. Joe
continued to sag on his knees, clutching his
wound, the twisted tail-plane hanging in
front of his face...

A fraction of a second existed between the
invisible roar of another Hurricane and the
sudden shape of the aircraft as it climbed the
slope and flashed into view, its Brownings
blazing from its angled wings. It began a tight
turn almost as soon as it came into sight,
diving a second time on the exposed German
infantrymen...

Squadron 2: The Sun Climbs Slowly

Matthew Holden

SEVERN HOUSE

First British hardcover edition published 1981 by
SEVERN HOUSE PUBLISHERS LTD
144–146 New Bond Street, London W1Y 9FD
by arrangement with Sphere Books Ltd

C0750327

18106639

ISBN 0–7278–0653–X

Printed in Great Britain by The Anchor Press Ltd
and bound by Wm Brendon & Son Ltd
both of Tiptree, Essex

For while the tired waves, vainly breaking
   Seem here no painful inch to gain
Far back, through creeks and inlets making,
   Comes silent, flooding in, the main.

And not by eastern windows only,
   When daylight comes, comes in the light
In front, the sun climbs slow, how slowly,
   But westward, look, the land is bright!

A. H. Clough, *Say Not the Struggle Naught Availeth,* quoted by Winston Churchill in his broadcast following the evacuation from Greece, April 1941.

ONE

A low continuous moan sounded from the jagged crack blown by the bomb in the Chelsea street. Anna Perowne stood behind the doctor who knelt beside the crater. Other men were squatting nearby, and the flickering from the flaming houses lit their pale, grimy faces as they peered into the narrow hole. Bombs had ceased to fall on West London, but Anna could hear dull thuds from the East. She smelt dust and soot and the sweat of the men in the rescue team as they carefully removed fallen debris in their attempt to reach the trapped Blitz victim.

The moan broke into a gurgle as the man's throat filled with blood. The doctor leant further over the pit, and Anna could see the swirls of dust caught in the thin beam of his torch as he tried to see below. He half-turned his head. 'Nurse — I'll need your help.' For a moment Anna failed to realize that he spoke to her, then she bent beside him. 'I can't reach down there,' he said. 'It's too narrow and too far, and we daren't move any more muck. You may be able to get to him, if we hold you.'

The doctor stood and stepped to one side; Anna edged forward; the hole opened black in front of her, and now the fearful gurgling sound was interspaced with whimpers.

'I'll try.'

'Good girl. We must give him a knock-out jab.' The doctor fumbled in his leather bag, then added: 'You'll have to go down head first. We'll hold your legs. Then your arms will be free. OK? Good. You'll have to take off that coat — and your skirt and shoes, otherwise they might snag the side and bring the lot down on you both.'

7

Numbly, Anna stripped. A burly workman took her clothes, and even in her fear Anna noticed the careful way in which his rough hands folded and laid the coat and skirt on the rubble. The draught from the burning houses dragged her slip against her legs as she stood beside the crater, and she could feel the heat of the flames warming through to her thighs. She knelt. The doctor passed her the syringe; someone put a torch between her teeth, hands grasped her ankles and calves, and she bent into the pit.

Anna worked her way down, one hand fumbling for the edge of the shaft, the other clutching the syringe. Her slip fell down over her waist as the men above dangled her deeper. The light from the torch knifed into the dark, then swung to the left as she moved her head, and found the remains of the man's face. A wave of sickness swept over Anna as she glimpsed the mess and the bubbles of blood issuing from what must have been his mouth, and she knew that if she failed to hold back her vomit she would drop the torch from her teeth. Her free hand touched the softness of the body; somehow she managed to give the injection, trying as she did so to remember the correct method which she'd only recently learnt at the first-aid classes. And then the hands began to pull her up again. Her hip caught against a small stone and it fell into the darkness below, landing with a soft thud, and Anna feared the entire shaft might collapse to trap her; her thighs, naked above her stockings, rubbed against the debris and she could feel the sting of the graze, then the warmth of the fire-swept Chelsea street struck her skin, arms took hold of her shoulders, and she sagged against the doctor, at last free to vomit. The burly workman spread her clothes over her legs.

'Well done miss. Here, have a drag.' Anna shook her head at the offered cigarette. 'We'll get some tea for you. Then we'll dig the poor sod out.' The workman flicked his cigarette into the dark and looked up into the sky, where searchlights still moved lazily backwards and forwards beneath the canopy of smoke and cloud. The man muttered: 'I'd like to know 'ow the buggers can get away with it. We do nothing to stop 'em – no guns, no RAF blokes, nothing. So they come and plaster us every sodding night.'

Anna stirred. She thought of the man below. And then she thought of Teddy and the rest of them in the Spitfire squadron, and her shoulders shook with her sobs.

Teddy Perowne searched for some object upon which to fix his eyes. He flew his Spitfire at 11,000 feet travelling at 200 mph. The three-quarter moon hung in the blue-black sky and reflected silvery on the clouds beneath Perowne's cockpit. He flew alone, having lost George and Joe as the section rose into the night from the misty airfield, heading for London. Now it seemed to Perowne that his flight must be endless; he travelled on and on, along a monotonous dim path between dark sky and pale clouds which seemed to lead to nowhere. He attempted to focus his tired eyes into the blackness, but failed since the lack of horizon denied him contact with the night world around him, and the stars which sprinkled the sky appeared for a moment to be moving whilst his Spitfire remained stationary, suspended in unearthly space.

And then the moving stars resembled the glimmer from aircraft, and Perowne's apprehension returned – over his lack of experience in night flying, over his realization of the Spitfire's inadequacies for night fighting, and beyond these reasons his nagging concern about getting home, knowing that soon he would have to sink into the clouds and deeper blackness in his search for the Kentish airfield. Perowne glanced at the dimly-lit instrument panel and checked his fuel, and calculated another ten minutes before he attempted to find base.

A glow became apparent beneath the Spitfire. Perowne eased his foot down on the rudder bar and banked slightly, looking to his right. The glimmer shone up through the thinning clouds, and Perowne realized that the light must be from burning London; the clouds broke for a moment, and he glimpsed the fires raging 11,000 feet below. The searchlights had ceased to probe; the bombers had gone, but the city continued to bleed, and Perowne imagined the pubs and the houses, and his own apprehension became swamped by his fear for Anna.

Perowne banked steeper into a circle and headed south for home. He could do nothing; nor could the rest of his squadron. Three days had gone since the first massive night-time attack on London on 7 September, and now the enemy seemed to be concentrating on these night strikes. Raids by day had brought further Luftwaffe casualties, but the after-dark bombers flew almost unmolested, and Perowne knew his pilots shared his own feeling of helplessness. He'd seen their faces when they returned from the night patrols – tense, eyes raw, angry – and he feared their frustration would lead them into making the mistake which would kill them. The squadron had suffered no losses since Chapman's death near Tonbridge on 6 September; pilot strength now stood at eleven with the latest three replacements, the highest it had been for many weeks. But Perowne's experience of these weeks had taught him that all could soon be changed, and the succession of comings and goings in the mess could accelerate into a blur of unremembered faces.

Barely three months had gone since the squadron first became operational. Of the nine pilots who had flown in those days of Dunkirk, only George and Joe and Perowne himself still fought; in many ways Perowne suffered greater fear for these two friends, despite their experience, than he did for the later arrivals. He depended upon them to a larger extent, and their death at this moment would seem an even more tragic waste, since the shift in Luftwaffe attacks from Fighter Command airfields to London allowed the squadron greater chance of survival. Yet Perowne knew that George and Joe, more than the others, shared his feeling of failure – George, normally so calm and calculating, had become slightly more reckless in his search for Luftwaffe night bombers. But at least the anger seemed to have swamped Joe's fear, and was honing the youngster's skill as a pilot into even greater brilliance. Perowne wondered for a moment how Simon would have reacted: Simon, always so cheerful and boisterous and strong, until his crash mutilated his face and body and destroyed his chances of further fighting.

Perowne checked his instruments again and gently pushed forward the control column. His Spitfire began to dip towards the clouds. He switched the R/T to transmit and called the airfield.

'Hello Zona. Hello Zona. This is Orange One. Request positioning. Am coming in.'

The voice of Control provided Perowne with a welcome contact with earth, yet at the same time increased his sense of isolation. 'Hello Orange One. Zona here. We have you Teddy. Steer 045 and hold for further instructions.'

The Spitfire slid into the clouds, leaving the beautiful, eerie worlds of moon and moving stars. Control guided Perowne down; he dropped beneath the clouds at about 2,000 feet, and Zona spoke again. 'Hello Teddy. The flare path will flash in seconds five.' Perowne searched below him, waiting for the momentary glimpse of the landing lights to lead him to safety, but the seconds sped by and the blackness remained unbroken. 'Hello Zona. I must be off course. I see nothing.' Fresh instructions sent the Spitfire curving further south. Now was the moment of greatest danger: around Perowne could be barrage balloons, and he feared his wings would be torn from the fuselage by a cable, and he wanted to pull back the stick to seek safety in height, but knew he must stay low.

For three tense minutes the Spitfire continued southwards. Perowne flew with his teeth unconsciously clenched, and the impenetrable wall of night crammed outside the cockpit seeming about to crush the frail machine. Then lights flickered ahead, for only five seconds but sufficient to open the wall, and Perowne hurried through his landing procedure. His voice over the R/T sounded as unemotional as ever, but his mouth relaxed, his staring eyes softened and his heart-beat slowed.

Another night mission was over, as futile as all the previous flights despite its dangers; Perowne's Spitfire touched the earth, and he wondered again how many hundreds of Londoners had died that night and if any of his pilots had been killed in the useless attempt to save them.

Joe lay in his bed. He could hear the gentle sound of breathing from the far side of the room where Phil Brookes slept in apparent peace; Joe still missed the raucous snores which had come from the other bed when Simon shared the room with him. Sometimes when he woke in the morning and fumbled into his flying jacket Joe still imagined Simon to be there, until he saw the newcomer's fresh, unstrained face on the pillow.

Only a few minutes before Joe had almost fallen asleep in his Spitfire as he flew above the clouds with the moon washing the interior of the cockpit. Now he felt as if sleep would never come. He shivered slightly and pulled the coarse RAF blanket tighter to his neck: the pre-dawn chill had struck into the Nissen hut, bringing with it a feeling of autumn. Joe's thoughts wandered to the fearful summer days which were now ending, days of sweating fear in the sunlit dogfights over Kent when he'd relied upon his beloved Spitfire and upon Simon's strength to see him through. Now his Spitfire lay a rusting wreck on the Foulness mud, and Simon fought to recover from his burns in a convalescent hospital; Joe would have to survive alone. Yet strangely he felt less fear since his props had been removed: terror had been to some extent replaced by the steady acceptance that each day might be his last.

At least Susie was safer. The shift in the Luftwaffe attacks meant less risk to the Kentish farm. Joe's thoughts flitted to the girl, and to the sunny days by the Medway when she'd helped him recover from his wounds and had tried to sooth his fears, and his mind concentrated on the image of her, with her sweetness and youth. Sleep finally filtered over the pilot; outside, grey light spread over the airfield, and mechanics readied the waiting Spitfires for another day.

'They haven't even any guns to bother about. The bastards can just fly where they like.' Osborne impatiently pushed his glass across the wet bar for another beer. The pilots were clustered in the mess; outside the weather had begun to improve after early-morning cloud, and the afternoon and evening promised to be clear – another fine night for the Luftwaffe.

George spoke, slowly and carefully as always. 'It's no good having anti-aircraft defences if we're in the same sky as the enemy. We'd be downed by our own guns.'

'But we can't do any good.'

George shrugged. 'There's nobody else.'

Perowne took his pipe from his pocket. 'It may be changing. Provisional orders have just come through from Uxbridge for tonight – we stay further south, away

13

from London. And there's been plenty of movement on the roads this morning. Something's being shifted. It must be the guns.'

Osborne turned to walk to a chair. 'Thank Christ for that. I've never felt so bloody useless in my life.'

Massed anti-aircraft batteries opened fire that night, spewing shells high above London. Anna waited at the Chelsea First Aid centre with other volunteer nurses, and to her the noise seemed shattering as the thump of the artillery shook the building and obliterated for a moment the grunt of distant bombs. She noticed the uplift in spirits of those sitting near her, and she felt a similar wave of emotion which almost amounted to relief: at last someone seemed to be hitting back. Immediately, she suffered a sense of disloyalty to Teddy.

Five minutes later Anna walked with the rest of her team down King's Road, and they passed an anti-aircraft battery: the gunners worked in their shirt sleeves, laughing and joking as they slammed the shells into the breeches. Anna stopped for a moment and she could see tiny bright red lights bursting way overhead, then the shrapnel clattered on the nearby roof-tops; the sound of cheerful singing came from the corner pub, and Anna remembered that the pub had seemed deserted the previous night.

But within half an hour the bombing appeared to be as bad as ever, despite the guns. Anna ran with the rest of her group first to a terraced house near Chelsea Embankment, where they tended to an old woman who lay on the pavement in her tattered nightdress and who seemed more concerned with her cat than with her own safety, then they hurried to Bramerton Street. There, amidst the swirling smoke and choking dust, she helped to search for victims in the remains of a large, once-elegant house. A man and a woman, husband and wife, had already been found dead, and soon afterwards the rescuers pulled out the body of a boy, their son. Another child, the 12-year-old daughter, was believed still to be buried. Anna joined the chain of men and women handing back bricks and debris, and the work continued after the guns had fallen silent and the Luftwaffe raiders had turned for home.

George's section managed to retain formation while the patrol continued just north of Canterbury. The three Spitfires flew V-shape, with the newcomer 'Handy' Andrews flying to George's port, and Joe to starboard weaving slightly behind. The pilots avoided all unnecessary talk over the R/T and each remained occupied with his own thoughts: George methodically worked out routes and heights which any returning Luftwaffe bombers might take, and hoped Control would direct his section accordingly; Handy flew with his fear thick in his gullet, certain he would never survive an encounter with the enemy and that even if he did, he would never be able to take his aircraft down through the dark to the safety of home; Joe concentrated on his flying and at the same time marvelled at the beauty of the clear night sky around him.

'Hello Yellow One. Zona calling.'

Joe immediately sat more erect at the sound of the Controller's voice: automatically, he checked the instruments in front of him, knowing that Zona was probably about to give instructions for an interception. He heard George's quiet voice. 'Hello Zona. I hear you.'

'OK Yellow One. Bandits approaching your location. Eight plus. Steer 090 degrees. Angels 15. They should be with you in about three, repeat three, minutes.'

'Roger Zona, moving now. Let's go Yellow Section. Line ahead.'

Joe eased in behind George's tail, hoping Handy would do the same with him. But after sixty seconds he

15

could no longer see the outline of George's Spitfire in the dark, and at the same moment Handy spoke over the R/T, his voice unnaturally breathless. 'I've lost contact. I can't see you.' 'OK Yellow Three. Don't panic. Just keep your eyes open for the bombers and for Christ's sake don't shoot us.'

The blindfold tightened around Joe's eyes as he flew onwards apparently alone. The three minutes must be finished; the bombers should be in the immediate area. He could see nothing but the stars and moon and the dark sweep of the sky, and the deeper blackness of the earth 15,000 feet below. Then, as he searched to his front, he noticed an object obliterating the stars only slightly higher than his own altitude. Joe pulled back the stick into a steeper climb. The shape began to pass him and Joe banked to follow, slipping off the catch to his gun yet wondering whether the other aircraft might be an RAF machine.

At that instant fire spat from the aircraft. Joe automatically slammed down on the rudder bar and thrust the stick forward in an avoiding movement, and at the same time experienced both astonishment and new fear. It was the first time he'd been fired on in the dark. He'd never realised what the effect would be — the fierce shower of illuminated bullets, some glowing red-hot, some whitish-green tracer, which scorched the blackness in a vivid line reaching towards him. Joe pulled back the stick again and searched the night above. Then he saw the dark shape once more blocking the stars, and he moved the control column further into his stomach aiming to rise beneath the enemy rear-gunner. He came up gently, almost floating towards his target. Suddenly he pressed his thumb on the firing button.

The effect of his own eight Browning machine guns firing into the night was even more startling than that of the enemy cannon. The night seemed to explode, with the Spitfire wings erupting into a line of flashing white which seared into Joe's eyes. Blinded by his own guns, he couldn't see the result of the three-second burst, and darkness fell again even blacker than before. Joe struggled to locate the enemy bomber, but failed even to distinguish the stars. He searched for five minutes, knowing almost from the start that the effort was wasted, and then he turned for home. He flew over Kent with his weariness chilling his body, and with his frustration stronger than ever.

Dawn had almost broken when the rescuers found the girl in the rubble of the Bramerton Street house. The news reached Anna while she sat clutching a mug of hot sweet tea, and she immediately hurried over the debris with the others. The girl lay trapped at the end of a long tunnel; someone had heard the sound of her sobs. It seemed impossible that she should still be alive, and equally impossible that the heaps of rubble could be moved to save her. An ARP man told Anna that a rubber tube had been pushed through the cracks to enable the child to drink tea; they might be able to widen the hole to allow food to be passed through.

Anna turned away to walk home; she wasn't needed for the moment. Her legs felt leadened and her arms ached with a pulsing throb. She looked up to see that the sky had brightened to pale green, and across it were the faint traces of vapour trails left by the departing German bombers, now being blown into ragged tendrils by the freshening dawn wind. From the west sounded a faint whine, growing stronger, and Anna peered upwards again. The hornet noise became louder, and now she could see four or five specks followed by others – a Spitfire squadron returning home, or perhaps embarking on another mission. Anna brushed back her dishevelled hair with her dirty hands, and she wished the pilots safety, then she continued to pick her way through the rubble and over the hoses which lay like massive snakes across the Chelsea street. She passed the anti-aircraft battery, noting the pile of used shell cases, and she wondered if the crews could claim any victims; she doubted it. The bombers seemed able to drop their death as easily as ever.

TWO

Perowne found his wife asleep on the bed. Anna lay fully-clothed, huddled with her knees up, her face pale, her long black hair strewn over the counterpane. Perowne looked down at her, then went to run the bath; he returned to wake her, kneeling beside the bed and smoothing his finger over the curve of her cheek, until her long lashes opened and recognition mixed with relief shone in her eyes. She opened her arms for him; he joined them round his neck and lifted her from the bed.

'Come on,' he said. 'The bath's ready. Then I'll tuck you in again.'

'Only if you come too.'

'Perhaps. Now just stand still.' Gently he undressed her, tossing aside the clothes one by one until she stood naked and beautiful before him; then he lifted her again and carried her through to the bathroom. He washed her slowly, and she lay obedient, smiling up at him.

Anna pushed aside her weariness when they came together in the bed, and the horrors of the past nights drove her even harder to find relief in the strength of his body. She welcomed his weight, and she bent her knees high on either side of him to allow him to thrust further. She sobbed: 'Deeper – oh please deeper.' And then she demanded him again, twisting over to mount and to ride him, her thighs gripping his chest and then parting wide as she threw back her head and came once more. She sat still for a moment, smiling down at him; he traced his fingertips over her skin, and she raised her arms to clasp her hands behind her neck, tightening her breasts against his gentle touch, still smiling down into his face.

19

He reached up suddenly to pull her down beside him. 'Now sleep,' he said.

'Will you stay with me?'

He nodded and grinned. 'But only if you leave me alone.'

'I promise. But not for long. I need you too much.'

Later he lay with his arms round her shoulders whilst she talked. 'They seem to be coming every night. I think the worst thing is that we can never see them. The bombs just drop from nothing. It's all so sudden, and so final, and there's nothing anyone can do to help themselves. I never knew it would be like this. It would all have seemed so unbelievable, even just a year ago. I still painted the same pictures, did the same things. Even when I started to go to the volunteer nursing classes it seemed unreal. And now this. It seems it'll go on forever, with nobody able to stop it.'

Within twenty-four hours orders reached Perowne that his pilots would concentrate again on daytime fighting. The Luftwaffe bombers would be left to the AA guns and to the pitifully few night-fighters. The decision seemed to Perowne to be an admission of defeat, even though he knew his Spitfires could do nothing against the night-time attacks. Group HQ at Uxbridge also warned that intelligence reports revealed considerable signs of enemy invasion preparations, and the attempt might be made at any moment. Osborne commented: 'They ought to try today — Friday the 13th.' George, sitting beside him in the Dispersal Hut, glanced up from the crossword and declared: 'There'll be no invasion. They'd be crazy to try now that autumn's coming. And one thing's for sure — the Huns aren't crazy.'

Perowne sat at the battered table, sheets of paper in front of him. His pencil scribbled names and numbers; he listed his pilots into groups, re-shuffled them, made fresh patterns, all in the attempt to spread his strength. His calculations formed a constant activity. George, who had acted as his second in command since the death of the New Zealander, Lex MacIntyre, joked about the Squadron Leader's preoccupation – 'you're always playing at God'. In one sense George was right: Perowne was always aware that the groupings he made might decide a man's life or death.

Each man depended on another, yet a wide difference in experience and capability existed amongst the pilots. George and Joe, and to a lesser extent Henny, Osborne and Peacock, had solid experience – the latter three had been with the squadron nearly a month now. So had Phil Brookes, who seemed to fly well enough but who always seemed so frail – Perowne felt some surprise that this youngster had survived so far. The latest four replacements were still novices – 'Handy' Andrews, Dunnet, Shaw, Lawson. The last two were Yorkshiremen and proud of it, and they'd already formed a team together. Dunnet was an equally proud Scot, but in a quiet fashion and Perowne found him difficult to assess. 'Handy' seemed keen to learn.

Clouds restricted air activity this Friday, with only single, tip and run raids. Perowne's squadron remained at Dispersal. But meteorological reports received later in the afternoon predicted that the weather might soon improve. According to the BBC news that night, heavy bombing attacks were being resumed on London; the pilots in the mess listened quietly to the BBC announcer and then continued their singing. Perowne walked outside and dimly he could see the glow to the north; the thud of guns sounded down-wind and aircraft droned monotonously in the background.

The 12-year-old girl still lay trapped beneath the ruins of her home despite rescue attempts throughout the day. Anna took her turn in helping during the evening until suddenly called away: a bomb had landed on an LCC

21

block of flats in nearby Flood Street. Anna ran along the road which alternately blazed with harsh light or lay shrouded in smoking, wavering shadow; she stumbled and fell and someone helped her to her feet again, shouting the need to hurry. Vaguely Anna heard the sound of whistling, and an explosion buffeted into her, but she kept on running.

Vast areas of glistening black water were spreading across Flood Street from a severed water main. Occupants of the shattered shelter were being helped out onto the pavement where some slumped to the ground, weeping hysterically; a doctor called to Anna, and she recognized him as the same whom she'd helped with the dying man in the fearful hole, but he didn't seem to recognize her in return. Together they administered to the shelter victims.

Miraculously, none seemed badly hurt. Many were suffering from shock, and all were filthy and sodden; some cursed continuously, others attempted to joke, others said nothing. Among those sitting silent was a boy in RAF uniform, his back against a wall and his eyes staring unseeing at the pool of water which lapped his feet. Anna squatted beside him.

'Can I get you anything? Do you need a doctor?'

He shook his head without looking at her and continued to sit as if stunned.

'You'd better not stay here. It isn't safe.'

The boy made no reply. Anna noticed the wings on his tunic. 'I see you're a pilot. Spitfires?'

'A Hurricane.' Suddenly he started to talk. 'They got my Mum and Dad. I only found out this afternoon. I came home to find it gone. Mrs Beck told me about it all. She lives next door. They died together, trapped in the bedroom. Martha Beck said they couldn't have lived long. I wonder who went first, him or her, and how long the other lasted afterwards.'

'Have you anywhere to go?'

22

'They were always so close. I'd like to think they went together. And they were so bloody proud of me being a pilot.'

'How old are you?'

'Nineteen. But I've shot down three.'

Anna felt as if far more than six years separated them. She wanted to hold him, like a child; instead she took his arm and pulled him to his feet.

'You mustn't stay here. Have you somewhere to go?'

'I suppose so. Yes. I've relatives down the East End – if they're still alive.' For the first time he looked at her. 'Thank you miss.' Then he turned and stepped off the pavement; Anna watched him walk down the road. She wondered if her husband's pilots were so vulnerable as he seemed to be, and how long the boy would survive, and if he became suddenly older when his Hurricane climbed into the sky.

Joe boosted his throttle to maximum speed. Ahead hovered the two Messerschmitt 111s apparently unaware of the approaching Spitfires. Joe settled himself more firmly in his seat, checking his mirror to see Dunnet reasonably close to his tail. He flicked the R/T switch. 'Keep with me Dunny. Guard my backside.' Joe bent forward and searched the sky above for signs of other enemy aircraft, squinting as he peered at the hazy sun. His actions formed part of the routine which he performed almost without thinking: his eyes skimmed the instruments whilst his fingers switched on the reflector sight and turned the trigger button from 'safe' to 'fire', and his mind was already calculating distances and deflection. The nearest enemy aircraft moved behind the small yellow electric-light dot projected by the reflector sight onto the windshield, with the target growing rapidly larger.

In those few seconds Joe's thoughts flashed through his mind in quick succession. He remembered the times

23

that he'd acted as Number Two to Lex, trying to stick with the reckless New Zealander, with Lex always plunging into the thickest of the fighting. He remembered his growing fear during those days, both for himself and his Spitfire, which had mushroomed into a conviction that soon he would die. He remembered the last time, following Lex out into the Thames Estuary after the crippled Dornier, and the sudden swooping enemy fighters, and Lex's final scream over the R/T admitting that he was as frightened as any man and didn't want to die.

This would be Joe's first real dogfight since that day, his first encounter with the enemy except for the night-time brush with the Heinkel. Joe realized that he felt no fear. His terror had been burnt away by the crash at Foulness after Lex's death; it was almost as if he had also died, and because of this could feel no further terror since his life could only end once. His quota had already been used.

Suddenly the Me 111 flipped sharply to port and fell into a steep dive. Joe's reaction was instantaneous: his foot kicked the bar and his hands pushed forward the stick, almost at the same moment that he'd seen the Messerschmitt wings begin to tilt. The two aircraft plunged together with the angle of their dives approaching the vertical. The fields and woods of East Sussex filled Joe's vision, screwing slowly to the right; the Messerschmitt moved into his sights again. He knew the enemy presented only a minimum target, but he nevertheless pressed the button. Almost immediately a huge chunk from the Me 111 hurtled up towards him, clattering off the Spitfire's starboard wing. The enemy aircraft twisted violently, smoke gushed towards Joe like a solid black wall through which he could see bursting flames, and he began to pull back the stick.

Violent thuds battered the armour plating behind Joe's seat. His aircraft vibrated viciously. He jerked the stick harder into his lap and the Spitfire's long nose soared skywards, and in the same moment Joe rolled to starboard to throw the aircraft into a controlled spin. The sudden switch thrust him harder into his seat and a mist slid over his eyes; he shook his head to clear his mind, straightened the machine and glanced to port and starboard: the second Me 111 was dipping far below him after having made its attack. Joe waggled the Spitfire's wings to check blind spots for other aircraft — he could see nothing, neither further Germans nor Dunnet who should have been protecting his rear. Perhaps the Scotsman was dead.

Joe located the second Me 111, speeding low towards the coast. He reckoned he might just be able to catch the enemy, using the speed from his superior height, and he dived in pursuit. The distance between the two aircraft gradually lessened. Joe glimpsed the houses of Battle below him, then he concentrated on the German aircraft hovering around the yellow dot on his windscreen. He fired, but the range was still too great and his tracer curved away beneath the enemy's belly. He closed and fired again, still without noticeable result and with the Messerschmitt now weaving to make itself a harder target. The two aircraft roared over Hastings and the beach. Joe pressed the button once more, only to find his ammunition expended, and he immediately banked back towards the shoreline. Beneath him the sea lay like polished silver in the noon-day sun.

He landed to discover Dunnet at the Dispersal Hut, slouched silent in one of the shabby armchairs. Joe asked: 'What on earth happened to you? I thought you were behind me.'

'I'm sorry Joe. I just couldn't keep up. You banked and dived so bloody fast that I lost you.'

Joe shrugged, loosening his Irvin jacket. It would do no good to say more, yet the thought nagged at him — how many of the latest squadron pilots were like Dunnet, with inadequate flying hours to protect both themselves and the others? A few minutes afterwards Joe learnt that 'Handy' Andrews had died, his parachute failing to open as he fell from his burning aircraft above Uckfield.

Two hours later Joe drove his motor-bike into the farmyard and propped the machine against the barn wall. He'd only seen Susie once since returning to the squadron after his crash, and that had been five days ago; now, after the excitement of the morning dogfight, he felt the need to be with her again.

He found her in the top orchard helping her twin brother to pick apples. Joe stood for a moment at the gate: Susie stood on the top rung of a ladder, wicker basket around her elbow, reaching high into the branches. As usual, she wore no shoes; she stretched on tip-toe, her fair hair catching the sun as it flowed down her back; she half-turned, and Joe could see the polished pebble necklace, which he'd given her for her eighteenth birthday when they'd sat beside the Medway that summer's afternoon. Joe could also see the firmness of her young breasts against the cloth of her dress, and the smoothness of her long legs, and the sight of her seemed to make him feel clean again.

Peter saw him first, calling out to Susie from another tree, and the puppy, Mops, ran bounding towards him. Peter immediately started to ask his usual questions: 'How many today? Why aren't you still at it you lazy blighter? Or are you leaving some for me?'

The three of them sat together in the shade of the apple-tree, Mops content with her head on Joe's knee, and Peter's pestering questions continued. Joe said: 'It was my first real dogfight since the crash.' He glanced at Susie: her large brown eyes were studying his face. 'How did you feel?' she asked.

'Fine. Honestly.'

'Of course he did Susie,' interrupted Peter.

'Somehow it feels better, having had that crash. I survived that so I reckon I'll survive anything.'

Susie abruptly changed the subject. 'How's Simon?'

'He's improving – at least his face and hands are, but he's still very low. I keep ringing the hospital. They tell me he's very depressed.'

'Perhaps I should go to see him again.'

'He'd like that.' Joe held out his hand to Susie. 'Come on – I'll help you pick the pippins, then perhaps you'll give me tea.'

Joe stayed at the farm until late evening, fussed over by Susie's mother and content to sit in the peaceful kitchen. Early in the evening the family heard the sound of aircraft; Peter hurried outside and called from the porch. Clouds had begun to gather but between the gaps Joe could see the setting sun glinting on bomber wings, and the drone continued high above before fading away to the north. More aircraft flew over an hour later and this time the noise of them reached down to rattle the kitchen windows. Susie shivered against Joe's shoulder and turned from the step to slip into the warmth again.

The first wave of bombers reached London soon after 5 p.m. Anna heard the air-raid siren as she stood painting in the attic studio at the flat; she put down her palette and moved away from the window, fearing glass splinters, but the first bombs dropped further east. She ran downstairs, pulling on her nurses' armband as she left the flat, then she hurried down the street towards the first-aid post.

Initial reports indicated heavy damage in the dock area. Then bombers began to probe further up the Thames. AA batteries in the Battersea and Chelsea area barked louder, seemingly with desperation, and the explosions started to thunder in the streets around King's Road. Only three minutes later a message reached the

27

first-aid post – another shelter had been hit, this time the crypt beneath the Church of the Holy Redeemer.

Rescue work had already begun when Anna reached the blitzed buildings, and she joined the others searching amongst the smoking rubble. The ARP man next to her had seen the bomb fall. 'It seemed to come at a slant through the stained-glass window, then blasted through the floor and into the crypt. God help the poor sods down there if you'll pardon my language.'

Anna stood back while workmen moved the last chunks of masonry covering the shelter entrance. Survivors staggered out, and then the stretchers were taken in; Anna watched, almost disbelieving, as the dreadful procession returned just in front of her: each stretcher was piled with remnants of women and children, some with a bloodstained sheet draping the bodies, others with the torn limbs visible.

'Come on nurse, we'll need you.' Anna followed the doctor into a nearby building. Trestle tables had been hastily erected, upon which were deposited the stretcher loads. Nurses and other volunteers were given their instructions. 'We have to piece the bodies together for burial. Don't try too hard – if you're too lavish with one body you might not have enough for another. Share it out a bit.'

Anna worked with the others until far into the night, and time became meaningless. The stretchers continued to arrive; the stench became gradually more appalling; efforts to create a decent individual body from the pile of severed limbs seemed increasingly hard. Anna fought against nausea and exhaustion. Her tears smeared the traces of blood and grime on her face and then dried stiff. The room in which she laboured appeared as a hell on earth, unreal and yet offering a warning of perhaps even worse horrors still to come. When Anna walked slowly home in the early hours of the morning she realized that this day was a Sunday. She stopped for a moment in

Bramerton Street, where rescuers were still attempting to reach the 12-year-old girl: incredibly, the child was apparently even cheerful as she waited for hands to lift her from her tomb. Anna walked on. She dreaded the dawn, since it merely heralded a day which would turn into another atrocious night.

Perowne walked across the grass to the Dispersal Hut, welcoming the fresh dawn air. Dew glistened on the wings of the waiting Spitfires; mechanics were already tinkering with the massive Merlin engines. Perowne checked his watch: 5.30 a.m. Light night cloud had almost evaporated, and the day promised to be sunny.

Perowne felt an unusual degree of anticipation, even greater than that before a normal day of fighting. This Sunday somehow threatened more. He remembered the Fighter Command Intelligence summary, dated the previous evening 14 September. 'Conditions indicating the imminence of invasion have increased ... A large number of barges has in the last three days moved southwards and westwards towards Ostend, Dunkirk, Calais and Boulogne. These movements, considered in conjunction with the increased scale of air attack on London, appear to indicate that attempt at invasion is likely. The enemy may merely be awaiting a suitable period of fine weather.'

Now the fine weather seemed to have arrived. Perowne also remembered the assessment given in the bar by George, with which he agreed. 'The Hun won't have much more chance before autumn weather wrecks any hope of getting over the Channel. They'll have to try soon, if they try at all. I don't reckon they will – but they'll do something.' And other intelligence reports had revealed a steady build-up in Luftwaffe strength on Belgium and French airfields, poised for intensified action.

The greater the threat, the greater the chance to hit

back against the agony being inflicted – if the squadron could survive the onslaught whatever form the assault might take. Perhaps this Sunday, 15 September, would be the day. Perowne entered the Dispersal Hut to join his waiting pilots.

THREE

'I hope the buggers come soon,' muttered Osborne, 'then we can be back in time for breakfast.'

Instead the wait continued, while the sun rose and the dew dried and the air hung warm and still. All ten pilots remained in Dispersal; after two hours food arrived from the mess, already cold on the trays, and the pilots shuffled round the table to eat. Osborne said: 'That bloody telephone will ring when I'm in the middle of this lot.' 'It couldn't taste worse,' said Henny, 'even if you had to leave it for an hour.'

But the telephone remained silent. Perowne noted that Phil Brookes barely touched his food, nor did Dunnet; the remainder seemed to eat well enough, and the two Yorkshiremen, Shaw and Lawson, grumbled for more despite Osborne's derisive comment that they must be pigs to enjoy the breakfast swill.

The pilots reacted to the continuing wait in their different ways. Phil sat in an armchair with a book, his slight figure almost hidden by the leather arms and his face seeming swamped by the bulky Mae West; Shaw and Lawson discussed cricket; Osborne and Dunnet played cards; Henny flicked backwards and forwards through a lurid magazine, his thin, peaky face peering at the pictures; Peacock slept outside in the sun. Perowne, Joe and George sat together in the doorway, with Perowne close to the telephone.

'Do you really think they'll come?' asked Joe.

George replied. 'They won't invade, but I still reckon we're in for a packet.'

Perowne nodded. 'The weather's too good. I don't know why they're leaving it so long.' He pulled back his Irvin jacket sleeve to look at his watch again. 'It's almost eleven. We've been sitting on our backsides for over five hours.'

Fifteen minutes later the telephone jangled on the wall. Perowne listened to the Controller's voice then slammed down the receiver, shouting: 'Scramble Orange Section. Let's go.' Joe was already sprinting across the grass and behind him ran the other four members of the squadron's first section – Osborne, Shaw, Lawson, with Perowne hurrying to catch up.

A flare rose lazily from the far end of the airfield; the Spitfires moved down the take-off path. Joe's nerves had ceased to flutter immediately he sat in the familiar cockpit. The Spitfire seemed an extension of his own body, and he handled the machine unthinkingly, correcting its peculiarities: as usual, the aircraft started to pull to the right during take-off, so he pressed the right rudder and added pressure with the left stick; the tail lifted and the nose no longer obstructed Joe's forward view; he eased the rudder to keep straight. Then he changed hands, flying with his left while he pumped up the landing gear with the right, and at the same time he glanced through the shimmering perspex before joining up with the others.

The section flew in V-formation southwards over the Downs, with Perowne leading, Joe on his immediate right as Number Two and Osborne outside him, and with Shaw and Lawson to Perowne's left. Osborne weaved slightly to the rear acting as rearguard. They climbed quickly, reaching 8,000 feet by the time they passed over Tonbridge and still rising.

Control came through. 'Hello Orange Leader. Reports are coming in of enemy groups assembled in Dieppe area and moving over the Channel. Believed groups comprise 40-plus, 20-plus and another 40-plus. Climb to Angels 20 and patrol Sector Charlie. Indicate when patrol line reached.'

The Spitfires continued their climb to 20,000 feet,

curving slightly eastwards over the rich fields of the Vale of Kent. Perowne reported their position; Control replied: 'OK Orange Leader. Liner, repeat Liner.' The section responded to the latest codeword by reducing speed to an economical level, and the pilots awaited further instructions. More information arrived three minutes later. 'Bandits 20-plus approaching Dover area.' And soon afterwards: 'Further 20-plus Bandits approaching Dover.' Almost immediately another command came from Control. 'Orange Leader. Vector Zero-Six-Zero. Buster repeat Buster.'

Perowne altered direction onto the new course and the pilots increased power to normal hull speed. Control informed the section that the enemy aircraft were heading towards Maidstone. Four minutes later Lawson's Yorkshire accent sounded over the R/T. 'Bandits! I see the sods. Below to port.'

'Tally-ho,' called Perowne. Joe saw the Squadron-Leader's Spitfire flip into a dive to the left, and he followed immediately; behind dropped the other three aircraft in line astern. Joe kept Perowne firmly in view; beyond he could see a formation of about ten Dorniers, with these bombers apparently unescorted by fighters — Joe searched about him for signs of Messerschmitts but could see nothing, and he readied himself for the strike. Ahead, Perowne began to level, coming flat towards the rear of the enemy formation, and fire from the last Dornier's cockpit was already floating upwards. Then Perowne dropped below the angle of the German machine-gun, and fire from his own Brownings streaked forward into the bomber's fuselage: Joe could see the flames glittering like a jewel necklace along the tail-plane and hull. Perowne curved to starboard, passing almost beneath the target; Joe followed him in. His gloved hand gripped the stick, his thumb pressed down, and the bullets licked into the wound which Perowne had inflicted. A sheet of flame suddenly wreathed the rear of the Dornier and Joe glimpsed the stricken bomber starting to spin. He pulled away to rejoin Perowne.

'Well done Joe. We got him between us.' Perowne's voice sounded matter-of-fact. Joe himself felt no exhilaration, merely as if he were performing some mechanical procedure. He rose to link with Perowne, and no sooner had he done so than the Squadron Leader dipped sharply into the attack once more.

This time they dropped beneath their second target until Perowne rose to rake the Dornier's belly. Joe had no need to contribute. Perowne's bullets found the enemy's bomb load; the aircraft disintegrated in a massive explosion. For an instant Joe feared Perowne might have perished in the blast, then he sighted the other Spitfire climbing beyond the smoke still under perfect control, and at the same moment Perowne's unemotional voice came over the R/T.

'That's it then. Fuel's getting low. Any signs of the other's?' 'Not since the first dive.' 'I daresay they'll find their way home. Let's refuel. I think it's only just beginning, Joe.'

They returned to find the second section already airborne. Mechanics rushed out to refuel and rearm the Spitfires, and the corporal who clambered onto Joe's wing shouted: 'There's a hell of a flap on. The Huns are coming over like bloody wasps.' More bombers were said to be making a landfall west of Dover, and the survivors of the original raid had zig-zagged westwards from Maidstone with some reaching London. Shaw and Lawson landed together soon after Joe and Perowne; a telephone message said that Osborne had come down at Biggin Hill, unhurt but with his aircraft badly riddled – he would make his own way back to the squadron.

Perowne, Joe, Shaw and Lawson scrambled again immediately their machines had been made ready. This time Control ordered them further north, towards the Thames Estuary: the bombers were still attempting to reach London, with fresh waves of small groups moving in scattered formations. Perowne increased speed as the four Spitfires climbed above the Kent hop-fields and over the sweep of the North Downs towards Dartford, and within minutes the Squadron-Leader could see the smudge of London's suburbs on the horizon. Smoke rose from the direction of Croydon.

The section approached the Thames, and ahead lay the balloon barrage, so thick that it seemed to form a line following the curves of the river, with all the balloons shining in the afternoon sun. Above were the tangled trails indicating dogfights already taking place, and over the R/T Perowne heard the chatter of other pilots engaging the enemy . . . 'Tally Ho!' 'OK Red Three – he's your's' . . . 'Diving now. Take your time.' 'Watch your rear, Alec.' And suddenly a scream. The calm voice of Control cut through the babble, ordering Perowne to lead his section into an interception further west, in the Greenwich area, and Perowne altered course in immediate response. Now the four Spitfires flew above London, over the myriad straight streets and terraced homes, and smoke curled towards them. Bombs were still bursting, sticks of them in almost instantaneous succession to the south of the loop of the Thames at Greenwich. And now Perowne could see the German raiders. He flicked his R/T.

'OK, Orange Section. Six Dorniers, same Angels as us, to the immediate front. We'll take them from the rear in a twin attack. Orange Three and Four to port.'

The Spitfires were closing fast. Shaw and Lawson moved up to the right, Shaw leading, and this second pair had barely time to draw level with Perowne and Joe before the Dorniers came within range. Shaw and Perowne opened fire at the same moment. The Dorniers immediately broke formation: one began to slant downwards, smoke fluttering gently from its starboard wing; four banked southwards, and even as they tried to escape

Perowne could see bombs dropping from their bellies. The last enemy aircraft maintained its course westwards towards central London; Perowne kicked the rudder bar to tilt his Spitfire in pursuit.

He could feel anger rising within him. He heard himself muttering 'the bastard, the bastard'. The Dornier still had a full load — 2,200 lbs of explosive ready to be dropped onto the city streets. Perowne boosted his throttle to the maximum, but the bomber had gained a lead and the range remained too great. Perowne could feel the sweat of rage on his face. He no longer flew without emotion: the vision of Anna flashed through his mind, and he fired an ineffectual burst which slid away well below the target, and he cursed his machine for moving too slowly. AA shells were exploding silently around him, but he scarcely noticed them nor his progress over London — below lay the green splash of the cricket ground at Kennington Oval, and still the chase continued.

Dimly Perowne heard Joe's voice. 'Orange Leader! Orange Leader! Teddy — for Christ's sake — Messerschmitts coming for your tail. Am going in. Break off for God's sake!'

Tracer flicked in front of Perowne's cockpit. His Spitfire shuddered as bullets shredded into one wing. But Perowne flew onwards, with the Dornier now growing larger in his sights.

'Teddy! I can't handle them alone!'

Bombs suddenly slanted away beneath the Dornier, plunging onto Battersea, and the enemy aircraft began to bank. Freed from its load, the Dornier increased speed as it sought to escape; Perowne rolled in pursuit, and at that moment his Spitfire's engine began to cough. He jerked his eyes from the Dornier down to the instruments and noted immediately the rising temperature; he throttled back into coarse pitch. Only then did Perowne's anger slide away, and he remembered Joe and the Messerschmitts, and he looked anxiously about him, seeing no other aircraft except faint trails to the south where dogfights still seemed to be in progress.

Perowne began to nurse his machine home. Departure of rage brought intense reaction. He knew that for the first time he'd lost control of himself: his anger, always rare, had caused him to throw aside judgement. And in doing so he'd not only risked his own life, but worse had possibly sacrificed Joe who'd been guarding his tail – in the past he'd condemned Lex for risking Joe with his recklessness, in just the way he himself had now done. And Joe might be dead somewhere in the streets of London, nor had his stupidity prevented the Dornier from unleashing its load.

The Spitfire engine started to stutter again. Perowne edged back the throttle still further and altered course for Croydon, with his injured aircraft dropping into a shallow dive towards safety. High above him the dogfight trails still twisted across the afternoon sky.

Joe thrust forward the stick into a pushover dive. The sudden negative-G caused the carburettor to cut; momentarily the Spitfire's engine stopped. Then the Messerschmitt's bullets crackled into the fuselage. Joe's legs were torn from the rudder bar and flung against his body and his knees folded up almost to his chest. He opened his mouth but no sound emerged. He fell forward on the stick, crashing his head against the column, and black clouds with twirling red circles jigged across his eyes as he fainted. The Spitfire picked up speed in the vertical dive. Then Joe heard voices on his earphones from the other dogfights – sharp commands, exhortations, curses – and the words provided him with some sense of normality. He wanted to say something over the R/T but lacked the strength. He felt in some bewildered way that he must keep holding the stick tight or it would float away from him and he would never catch it again.

The feel of the metal in his gloved fingers became more tangible. He realized that his grip offered his only hope of safety and that his aircraft was diving and must soon smash into the ground. Slowly he began to straighten his legs and ease his body back in the seat, taking the stick with him, fighting against the power of the Spitfire as its determined dive to death continued, and gradually succeeding. The horizon floated into his vision, and an increasing area of sky, and the aircraft slowly levelled.

But the Spitfire still shuddered – huge vibrations which threatened to tear the machine apart. And Joe could smell acrid burning, and could feel the heat through the thick soles of his flying boots. The aircraft would soon explode, and already black smoke had started to fill the cockpit. Joe's mind had cleared, and he acted calmly and methodically: he lifted his seat, unplugged the R/T and oxygen, undid the harness, slid back the hood, then kicked on the rudder bar to roll the aircraft onto its back and to drop into space.

The blast of the bomb caught Anna as she ran for the shelter. She heard nothing, nor did she feel the impact, simply a sensation of falling into a huge pit. Then she became aware of the body beneath her. She tried to move and found herself pinned by someone lying across her thighs; she coughed and began to retch as the dust clogged her throat. Her legs were suddenly freed and hands grasped her arms to pull her up. Someone shouted close to her ear: 'You all right love?' She nodded, trying to wipe the dirt from her eyes, and then she saw the blood on her hands and across her coat, and she looked down at the body on the pavement in front of her upon which she'd been sprawled. Huge wounds gaped over the man's back and his head appeared half-severed.

'I reckon he saved you love,' said the voice in her ear again. 'He caught the splinters, poor blighter. Here, come on, let's see about a mash of tea for you.' Anna followed the ARP warden; it seemed wrong that she could walk away unharmed whilst the remains of the man lay on the pavement, his blood still wet and his body still warm, and his hat still clutched tight in his clean white hand.

The telephone rang in the Croydon mess. An orderly approached Perowne, standing alone and still numb at the bar. 'It's for you, sir.' Perowne picked up the receiver.

'Teddy?'

'Joe! God it's good to hear you.'

'They told me at the airfield that you'd had to stop off at Croydon.'

'Where are you? Are you OK?'

'I'm fine. I baled out over Crystal Palace. I'm at King's College Hospital – nothing serious, just a twisted ankle. I landed in a blasted dustbin. Made an awful row.'

'Joe, I shouldn't have gone haring off like . . .'

'Forget it. I understand. I must leave you – just wanted to know you were OK. Now I'll find a bed somewhere – I'll never get back tonight. You'll have to manage without me.'

'Joe – ring Anna. I'll give you the number. She can put you up. It'll do her good to see you.'

Joe hesitated. 'Well, I don't know. Are you sure it'll be OK?'

'Of course it will. You can look after her for me.'

Joe reached the flat soon after the all-clear. Gangs of men were still working in the rubble-strewn Chelsea streets, and Joe had witnessed similar sights in his taxi-ride across London. His driver maintained a cheerful chatter as he sought detours round the blocked roads. 'Good for business this, mate – puts no end of mileage on the clock. How're you boys doing anyway? I reckon you've the best job – must be as safe as houses up there, if you know what I mean.'

39

Anna opened the door almost immediately Joe started to ring, as if she'd been standing waiting for him. He felt nervous, and wished he hadn't come, yet Anna had seemed pleased when they'd spoken on the telephone. Now she kissed his cheek, holding him lightly for a moment, and Joe felt the softness of her hair against the bruise on his face.

She pulled away, smiling, and gently touched the plaster across his temple. 'Come on, I'll help you up the stairs. You must be careful with that ankle.'

'It's fine really. It was such a damned silly thing to do, landing in a dustbin. Not very dignified. The lady who lived in the house had to help me out — she kept apologising because the bin was full. I said it would've hurt even more if the thing had been empty. Then she stuck me in a chair in her front room and insisted on filling me with weak tea till the ambulance came. I ask you — one minute you're up there keeping the Germans company, and the next you're being entertained to tea by a dear old lady, having to admire her aspidistra and her ancient wedding photographs.'

'I promise you I won't show you our's.'

They ate in the living room, with Anna sitting on the floor and Joe on the sofa. Joe felt the ache fading from his head. He continued his attempt to cover his nervousness by talking, and gradually he felt at ease. He talked about the squadron, but never about the fighting, only about the horse-play in the mess; she told him of her attempts to be an amateur nurse, but nothing of the horrors which she'd witnessed, only the miraculous escapes. 'There's been a 12-year-old girl buried in Bramerton Street for five nights. They've just got her out — and she's going to be fine.'

Joe watched Anna's face while she talked, first shyly then with greater confidence. Her tiredness seemed to emphasise her dark beauty — the depth of her eyes, the pale skin. His consciousness of her as a woman became

40

increasingly powerful, and his eyes moved to the curve of her thighs as she sat on the carpet with her legs bent up, and to her long fingers as she clapsed her hands around her knees.

'How old are you Joe?' she asked suddenly.

'Twenty.'

She smiled. 'Not very old.'

Joe grinned in reply. 'Depends what for. It seems old enough for this business. Mind you, I'm not an old man like Teddy.'

'Old man indeed. He's the same age as me, twenty-five. Does that make me an old woman?'

'Hardly.' The difference in age increased her attraction, as it did with Susie in reverse: Susie seemed so young, and fresh and clean, while Anna held a woman's promise.

'How's Susie?'

'She's fine.'

'I'd like to see her again. I've only met her twice, and both were a bit grim – the first when Teddy came to tell you about Simon, and then when we visited you in hospital. She's very beautiful.'

'I know.'

'I'd like to paint her – a portrait and a full-length. Do you think she'd mind?' Joe shook his head.

Later Joe lay in the bath, the water shallow yet sufficient to soak the weariness from his body and the ache from his ankle. Anna's presence seemed strong in the room – the cosmetics beside the basin, the wrap behind the door. Lying there naked, Joe's desire began to grow. The bath beneath him had last touched her body; the long mirror on the wall had last reflected her nakedness as she stepped from the water; the towels which she'd given him had moved over her skin. He noticed the door lacked a lock, and this deliberate neglect stimulated him still further – there seemed to be no obstacle between them: the door could open and she could enter and be with him.

41

Joe slept on a mattress on the floor of the attic studio. The night sky remained quiet. Sleep came over him as soon as he closed his eyes, obliterating his memories of the dangers of the day, and soothing his desire for the woman who lay in the room below.

Anna lay awake, too tired to sleep. She listened for the sound of aircraft, but it seemed as if the Germans had expended all their energy during the day. Her mind kept returning to the sights she'd seen, and to the mutilated corpse which had cushioned her body on the pavement with its raw wounds and its horrible contrast of humanity and butchery. Anna forced her thoughts away, and they came to rest on Joe.

He wanted her. She'd been aware of his need and his longing for the comfort of her body. And with her thoughts, Anna could feel her own longing beginning to surge into desire. He lay near, and naked: he'd refused a pair of Teddy's pyjamas saying he'd rather do without. 'Usually I have to sleep in my clothes – the whole damned lot. It'll be grand to feel free.' Now Anna imagined his body, stretched in sleep, firm, clean from the bath, between the sheets which had previously covered her own body, his skin ready for her touch. Slowly Anna moved her hands down beneath the bedclothes to smooth them over her limbs: she pushed her nightdress higher to touch her breasts, and her caress tightened the skin, then her fingers moved lower; her hips slowly began to rotate, and her breathing quickened as she sought her own relief from loneliness and from the horrors of the day.

Starlings woke Joe as they quarrelled in the early morning sun on the tiles outside the studio window. He lay content, savouring the difference between this room and the harsh quarters at the station. He smelt turps and linseed oil; around the walls were propped paintings, and an unfinished canvas remained on the easel: Anna painted boldly, with strong brush-strokes and vivid

42

colour, rich with a feeling of warmth and life. One canvas was of a nude woman, her back half-turned towards the painter; her breasts were hidden and yet the girl's slender back and firm hips were even more sensuous than if she were fully exposed, and the expression on the face made it appear that the girl was looking at her lover, rather than at another woman. Joe remembered that Anna wanted to paint Susie, and he wished it could be done soon.

The door to the studio opened quietly: Joe hadn't heard Anna's footsteps on the stairs.

'Did I wake you?'

He shook his head. 'I was only dozing.'

She stood in the doorway for a moment, holding a tray and with her deep red housecoat reaching to her bare feet. 'I've brought some tea. I have to be leaving soon — I'm on nursing duty in case there's another raid.' She walked forward and knelt to place the tray beside the mattress on the floor. 'Stay as long as you like — let yourself out. How does your ankle feel?'

'Fine I think. And my head. I'm fit to fly again. And if it's anything like yesterday they'll need me back.'

She still knelt looking down at Joe. His dark curls were tousled and his face had the freshness of sleep. Soon he would be fighting again, and soon she would be in the Blitz again, and the peaceful sunlit room would be changed to a hell for both of them. Joe's blue eyes were watching her own, then she saw them fall to her neck and lower to the housecoat and to the glimpse of the nightdress beneath. Slowly she reached towards the sheet which covered his naked body; she started to smooth the sheet as if she were merely tidying the bed around him, until her fingers touched the skin of his shoulder, and there they rested. She could see that his breathing had quickened, and his eyes were on her face again. Her fingers began to slide beneath the sheet, feeling the warmth of his chest.

Suddenly Anna bent forward to kiss the exposed

43

shoulder and she kept her head resting on his chest as her fingers pushed lower to the flatness of his stomach. She crouched there, on her knees, in a position of almost supplication, and she could feel his arm come around her shoulder.

Joe felt the quivering of her body, and the softness of her breasts against him, and the firm nipples through the cotton of the nightdress. Her hand rested on his stomach, finger-tips reaching to the hair below.

Their embrace brought no sense of disloyalty, either to Teddy or Susie, and guilt would still have been absent if her fingers had moved lower to his hardness and if their bodies had come together. Their needs were even more basic than those of lovers. Day by day Joe only touched those things which were harsh and hard – the cold metal of the control column in his Spitfire, the roughness of his flying boots, the rigidity of the earphones clamping his head and the oxygen mask encasing his face. Now he could feel Anna's suppleness and warmth, and he knew her limbs would yield to him, opening the way to the softness between her thighs. Anna sought the reverse. Daily she witnessed the frailty of existence – the bodies blown suddenly to nothing, the abruptness of death, the absence of protection, the inhumanity whereby one man could act impersonally high in the sky and could destroy men, women and children without discrimination, and with the victims dying in the most personal and undignified way possible; Anna had yet to reconcile herself to the fact that an unseen, unknown person sought to kill her, for no reason. Life seemed so intangible. But now, beneath her, lay the strong body of a man, supremely alive and with the masculine hardness of desire. She wanted him to thrust his life into her; she wanted to clutch him with her fingers and with her body. He had both the appeal of a man and a boy: the first offered masculine strength, the second a promise of the future.

But then Anna felt Joe's heart beating against her

breast. The movement reminded her of a fluttering moth, which she'd caught in her cupped palms so that she could allow the insect to escape the light. Joe's heart was equally fragile. All depended on that tiny pulse; his solidity was an illusion.

Anna stirred to look into Joe's eyes; she smiled sadly and simply shook her head, and she knew he understood. Softly and slowly she kissed his lips, her hair falling forward about his face. She knelt back on her heels, taking his hand and placing it on her breast whilst she traced her finger-tips over his mouth and bruised cheek and tired eyes, then she rose to go.

FOUR

Dunnet had died the previous afternoon, his departure dismissed in one sentence when George told Joe the news: 'He tried to outdive a Messerschmitt coming down behind him and any fool knows the 109 is faster than a Spit in a dive.' Peacock was missing, and by now hopes were slim for his reappearance; Phil Brockes had been shot in the leg and would be unable to fly for at least a month. Squadron strength was therefore down to seven.

Perowne joined George and Joe at the bar. So far the day had been quiet; rain beat against the mess windows and low cloud hung over the airfield. 'I think they'll stay away today,' said George. Perowne commented: 'They need to, after yesterday. It seems the whole Luftwaffe was knocking at the door. It must've been their biggest effort yet.' Perowne had just received the official casualty figures for 15 September – 186 enemy aircraft shot down, plus 46 probables and 72 damaged; Fighter Command losses were said to be 25 aircraft, with 13 pilots killed or still missing. According to the Air Ministry statement: 'The fighting of the previous day was most successful. The enemy adopted bolder tactics; these served only to increase his losses. The figure of enemy bombers destroyed was very striking.'

'I don't believe it,' said George. 'We didn't shoot down that many – couldn't have done.'

'They must have taken a hammering,' argued Joe.

'So did we. Three pilots gone, probably two for good. Just in one bloody afternoon. The youngsters never get enough flying hours to give them a reasonable chance.'

'Perhaps they soon will,' said Perowne. 'I've good news for you. The squadron is being shifted up north on the 18th — we're due for a rest. And we'll be getting new Spits — the Two A. I heard this morning.' He pushed forward his glass to be refilled. 'So we all go on holiday — if we can last another forty-eight hours.'

Perowne placed Joe 'off-state' for the rest of that Monday to allow his ankle to recover. He himself flew in the afternoon, leading his section comprising Shaw and Lawson and with Henny his Number Two. The weather improved but Control reported only small enemy groups coming towards the south coast and these were intercepted by squadrons operating from the forward airfields; Luftwaffe attempts to reach Detling and Biggin Hill were mainly ineffective, and Perowne's patrol returned without being involved.

Joe remained in his room, reading and welcoming the solitude provided by the absence of Phil Brookes. The youngster still seemed alien after Simon. Phil was so damned tidy, thought Joe. In all ways he amounted to the direct opposite of Simon — self-effacing as opposed to Simon's boisterous boasting, unnaturally quiet, almost finicky in his personal cleanliness, abstemious. Suddenly Joe swung his legs from the bed and limped to the telephone in the corridor.

'Mr. Barrett. It's Joe — yes, I'm fine thank you. Can I speak to Susie? ... Susie. Can you come with me tonight? I'd like to see Simon. Would you mind?'

The convalescent home lay hidden by beeches in the woods near Farnborough. Joe cut the motor-bike engine beneath the trees and helped Susie from the pillion, holding her hand for a moment to warm her chilled fingers.

'Are you nervous?' he asked.

'A little.'

'So am I. That's why I wanted you with me.'

'Do you think he'll see us?'

Joe shrugged. 'I don't know. That's why I haven't rung, so that he couldn't say no. They've told me before that he's still very conscious about his face. And he's still terribly angry that they won't let him fly.'

A nurse told them they would find Simon in the bar. 'That's where he spends most of his time. We don't let them drink much, but he makes his last.' They walked down the carpeted corridor. All the patients they passed grinned at Susie; most were heavily bandaged, though some had their facial wounds exposed, and Joe could feel Susie's hand gripping tight around his arm.

Simon saw them as soon as they entered the square, high room. His face was partially covered by a thick plaster extending from his neck up his right cheek; his hair grew in patches and the naked skin above his forehead seemed ghastly white in contrast to the burnt tissue around his left temple. A small plaster partially covered the space where his nose had been. He stood from his stool as they approached and his slight smile reminded Joe painfully of the broad grin which used to spread across his friend's face.

'I'm honoured,' he said.

'Did you mind us coming?'

'I don't suppose so. You've both seen me before. I just don't like seeing strangers and the look on their faces, and their blasted pity – I'd rather they vomited at the sight of me.' He took Susie's hand. 'You get prettier each time I see you. I'd kiss you if I didn't look such a mess.'

Susie reached up quickly and touched his left cheek with her lips. Then she smiled and said: 'You never were much to look at – you said that yourself once.'

They sat and talked, with Simon insisting on hearing all the squadron news, and Joe welcomed his questions as a sign that Simon might be emerging from his depression. He told him of the recent heavy fighting and the losses suffered by the squadron, both in pilots and aircraft, and how the replacements seemed younger and more in-

48

experienced each time. 'They make me feel very old,' he said. Simon answered: 'And so you are. You've lived since Dunkirk and that's a hell of a time. You lived longer than me.'

'You're still around.'

'Christ — you don't call this being alive.' Simon suddenly added: 'Susie, you shouldn't have come with Joe tonight.'

'Why not?'

'Because you look too damn good together, the pair of you, and you make me feel even sorrier for myself. Stick to her Joe — she's better than you deserve.'

Joe waited with the other three pilots at the Dispersal Hut next morning and wondered why his anticipation seemed even greater than usual: he felt more tense, and although he knew that his nerves would suddenly steady when he sat in the cockpit, he still couldn't define the cause for his added anxiety. Then Shaw commented: 'It would be a right bugger if I got clobbered today, when we pack up tomorrow.'

Ten minutes later the telephone shrilled. Shaw, Lawson and Osborne were almost out of the door when Joe replaced the receiver and called: 'Forget it. We stay put for a while — there's nothing doing. There's still nine-tenths cloud cover over the coast. But it's expected to clear.'

The pilots waited. Drizzle swept across the airfield in misty curtains and the rain dripped steadily from the corrugated iron roof of the Dispersal Hut. The sound of the water-drops plopping into the butt by the door became an irritant, rubbing the raw nerves of the men inside the building. Osborne suddenly swore and began to pace the room; Lawson snapped at him to stay still, and Shaw joined in the subsequent bickering, siding with his friend. Joe walked outside and stood on the step, welcoming the cool moisture which settled softly on his skin; his ankle still ached slightly and he wondered if it would pain him if he had to stamp hard on the rudder bar – he would probably never even notice. Then Joe glanced to the south and saw the lightening sky, and at that moment the telephone jangled again.

The section emerged from the clouds at 6,000 feet to find the sky arching above them, shimmering blue and beautiful. The sun streaked into Joe's cockpit, warming his cheeks and soothing the stiff muscles. He immediately pushed the R/T switch. 'Hello Yellow Section. Watch that sun for Huns.' The section continued to rise; Joe's apprehension remained, since he knew the black outlines of the Spitfires would be easily seen against the white clouds below.

Five minutes later, Control issued instructions. 'Continue your climb Yellow Section. Bandits approaching at high altitude, estimated Angels 25. Maintain your present course and speed. You should have them in view in approximately seven minutes.'

Joe and his pilots located the high-level vapour trails earlier than estimated. The Spitfires were still climbing, and to the north Joe identified another Spitfire formation also reaching upwards; the R/T informed him that more Fighter Command squadrons were converging for the interception. The dots became larger at the head of the trails and gradually took shape – Dornier 17s and 215s – and other specks could be seen flying even higher, probably escorting fighters. The bombers were heading north-east in V-formations each of about fifteen machines. Joe selected a group on the western fringe of the enemy wave.

The section approached from the front at a slanting climb. Joe issued a last warning to the other three pilots: 'Watch out for the fighters dropping down on us' and then the guns beneath the leading Do-17 began to fire. Joe watched the silent streaks floating towards him then rushing above his canopy. The shape of the Dornier seemed to fill his sights; he pressed down his thumb and the shape of the enemy suddenly blurred with the vibration from his Brownings. He rolled to starboard and into an inverted loop so that he could strike up again, and now the sky was crammed with rushing aircraft and criss-crossed cannon fire in the frenzied inferno which he knew so well.

Even amidst the confusion Joe repeatedly glanced at the enemy fighters at the higher altitude: the Messerschmitts had still to commit themselves to the dogfights around the Dorniers. Joe no longer had any idea of the whereabouts of the rest of his section, and could only hope that they were fending for themselves and that Osborne was somewhere close to him defending his tail. He continued to tear into his Dornier victim: three times he struck from below the bomber, each time flying through the flailing bullets, and after the third attempt the bomber began to lose height. Now Joe approached from above and behind. Fire from the enemy machine guns had become intermittent, and he guessed that at least one of the gunners had been killed.

This time Joe's fire ripped along the length of the slim fuselage before curving away just behind the square cockpit. The Dornier dipped lower. Flames sprouted from the aircraft's body in the region of the ugly black cross behind the Dornier's wing, and as Joe dived again he could see the fire spreading forwards, without smoke and licking hungrily towards the cockpit. He passed close above, and saw the white upturned faces of the men behind the squat canopy; he banked into a climbing circle and waited to see if the crew baled out, but they seemed to be making no attempt, and he plunged again to commit the final act. Even before he reached his target, the Dornier exploded: one wing hurtled sideways to port, and the remainder of the wreck slipped to starboard with the intact wing pointing the way towards the distant earth.

51

The bomber began its leaf-like spiral with Joe following it down, and still no parachutes appeared.

A film seemed to fall across Joe's eyes as his Spitfire dropped after the doomed Dornier. Dimly he'd already noticed the black smudge which had appeared on the edge of the perspex in front of him, but his preoccupation with killing the enemy had prevented him from taking real notice. Now the smear was widening rapidly as oil leaked from the engine and sprayed upwards to the windscreen. Joe checked the instruments, which registered the pressure change, and he eased back the throttle. Gradually the clouds rose up to meet him, first a solid mass then with the valleys and drifting peaks becoming more closely defined; Joe dipped into a snowy trough and then slid deeper into the mist, and the whiteness enveloped him. He broke from the cloud at 3,000 feet almost above Maidstone, and he began to follow the railway line leading westwards towards home. By now the black curtain across his windscreen was impenetrable: he found his way by banking his aircraft first to port and then to starboard as he viewed the ground below.

He sighted the familiar beech woods and the open grass and he began his approach. He came down almost blind but nevertheless touched firmly and with confidence. Tiredness suddenly swept over him as he taxied towards Dispersal, and the ache in his ankle returned stronger than ever. He wanted to drop his chin to his chest and to sleep; his aircraft moved steadily forward. He noticed a Spitfire tilted at a crazy angle beside the field and he recognised Osborne's number: the pilot was standing beside the wrecked machine talking to ground crew. Joe brought his aircraft to a halt and cut the engine, with the silence buffeting into him and with his weariness seeming almost a physical pain. A mechanic slid back the oil-stained hood and helped him unbuckle the harness; he took the man's hand as he clambered onto the wing, and

52

when he jumped to the grass he felt his knees would give way beneath him. He stood for a moment, looking at the dirty, battered Spitfire.

'That's the fourth bloody oil leak in the last three days,' grumbled the mechanic, already tending to the engine. Joe turned to sling his parachute on the wing and to walk back to Dispersal; the hut seemed too far away. Shaw and Lawson were already there, both slumped with their backs to the wooden wall of the hut, cigarettes dangling from their fingers.

Aircraft and pilots were exhausted; the limits of endurance for machines and men had almost been reached. But Joe suddenly realized with a sense of astonishment that now he would survive for a while and could try to recover before battle closed around the squadron again.

Lapwings wheeled and soared above the airfield on the edge of the Yorkshire moors. The birds had been performing their aerial acrobatics throughout the morning, twisting and twirling, the September sun catching the white of their bellies and the black sheen of their ragged wings; their peculiar shrill mewing had been a constant sound, drowned only by the angry roar of the Spitfire engines being tested in the nearby hangar.

Joe lay on the grass, watching the birds and envying them their flight. Shaw squatted beside him; he said: 'The old 'uns are teaching the youngsters. Soon they'll be gone off to the coast, but they'll be back come spring.' Lawson added: 'It's a pity we're not here in breeding time – the eggs taste damn good.'

Perowne put down his book and glanced at his watch. 'OK you three. It's time for lessons.' They walked towards the airfield buildings, their half-zipped flying boots flapping clumsily about their calves, parachutes dragging heavy in their hands, and the lapwings continued their effortless rising and falling above them.

Outside the hangar stood the bright new Spitfire, the camouflage paint without blemish, the metalwork untarnished, the wings free from traces of soot from guns. The other four pilots were already waiting by the machine – Phil Brookes, who had only returned from hospital three days before, still needed the support of his crutches.

The neat-uniformed Sergeant began his lecture, his voice brisk and the content spoken by him many times before. 'Now this, gentlemen, is the Mark Two A. I'll explain the main differences to the Mark One which you've been flying, and I'm sure the improvement will be appreciated. ... The powerplant is the Merlin 12, developing 1,150 horse-power, as opposed to 1,030 with the Merlin 2. Maximum speed is in the region of 357 mph, rather than the slightly faster 365, but you have a more rapid rate of climb – 2,600 feet per minute. The service ceiling is pushed from 34,000 to 37,000. Aircraft dimensions and fuel range remain the same.' The Sergeant walked to the wings. 'You'll see the difference in the armaments, giving you greater punch. You now have four .303 Brownings, rather than eight, but instead you also have the two 20mm Hispano cannon, and I believe you'll be very pleased with them in your bomber interceptions...'

Perowne scarcely listened. More power, more strength – both were very fine, but they did nothing to solve his problem of gaining pilots with sufficient experience to fly the new machines. Indeed, the improvements might initially make even greater demands on the newcomers. The squadron was still well below strength: Peacock had never returned from the dogfights on 15 September, and was considered officially dead; Brookes would be unable to fly for another month. Perowne, therefore, had an effective strength of seven pilots rather than the official establishment figure of at least twelve.

Five newcomers would be arriving next day, the

largest single batch of replacements that the squadron had ever received. But Perowne doubted the quality of the expected arrivals: most likely they would be younger than ever, with only a minimum of solo flying hours and with only a handful of these in Spitfires.

Perowne reckoned he would have about two months to bring his squadron into effective shape again. The pilots had been in Yorkshire for three weeks, and Perowne had tried to allow them as easy a time as possible even though, as part of Catterick sector in Number 13 Group, they had to be ready to block infrequent raiders coming across the North Sea from Norway. So far the squadron had only been called out once, six days ago on the first day of October when very high altitude bombers had been detected heading for Scotland, but these were intercepted further north by Hurricanes from the Wick and Turnhouse sectors.

In some ways the boredom was even worse than the fighting. The pilots could never be free from the expectation of combat; nerves were still raw; they remained 'on state'. After the first few days of calm, Perowne noticed his men becoming increasingly restless. They kept hearing reports of fighting further south – although this had diminished dramatically after the huge battle of 15 September – and they felt they wanted to belong to it again, especially since London was being hammered by the night bombers. This thought pulled Perowne's mind to Anna. He rang her as often as he could, and she tried to be cheerful, yet many times he telephoned and the instrument kept on ringing, and in those dragging moments he felt sick with fear. He wanted to be with her again but she refused to come to him. 'No darling,' she'd said the previous night. 'I don't want to be a coward. Besides, you'll be coming back before long.'

Another two months without her, except perhaps for a snatched leave. Perowne felt isolated, caged with his squadron on the edge of the Yorkshire wilderness, in a small, introverted masculine world of pilots and aircraft and beer and discussions of tactics.

The Sergeant finished his lecture and answered questions, then discussed with Perowne the allocation of the new machines which would be arriving over the next three days. Perowne stood alone for a moment, looking at the Spitfire in front of him. He'd never been able to form an attachment for the aircraft he flew, unlike the close emotion which he knew Joe had once felt for his aeroplane, and this machine seemed a stranger. He turned to join the others in the bar.

Joe rose above the airfield and gloried in the Spitfire's strength. He continued to climb towards the sun, welcoming the dazzling rays, knowing that for the moment he could fly safe from enemy fighters lurking in the blinding light. He boosted the throttle, and well within ten minutes had risen to 20,000 feet; then he levelled, feeling the ease with which the Spitfire responded, before turning the aircraft into a leisurely roll and a huge inverted loop. He pushed the stick forward into a shallow dive and as he did so the Yorkshire horizon opened before him: the rich tan fells sweeping inland from Richmond and onwards into the crumpled green folds of the Dales – Swaledale and Wensleydale and onwards into the hills. Beyond lay the Lake District, and his home, and Joe experienced a sudden longing to be there.

Reluctantly he banked for the airfield. He wanted to stay aloft, savouring the joy of flying away from all thoughts of fighting. The aircraft didn't seem to be a weapon: it lacked the stink of combat, the perpetual odour of sweat and cordite and over-heated oil. His contentment and pleasure prompted fanciful thoughts: he wondered if Susie would enjoy to fly as much as he did, whether she would want to smile with sheer delight, whether she would feel the urge to continue upwards reaching for the sun. No – Susie belonged to the earth.

Her brother Peter perhaps — he was eager enough to join.

The newcomers who had arrived that morning were barely older than Peter — less than two years younger than Joe himself, but those intervening months, and especially the last year, set a great gap between them. Now Joe would have to try to teach them how to survive, and he wondered if any of them would reach his own age.

Mock dogfights swirled above the fells. The aircraft were divided into pairs, and to Perowne they seemed to be performing a weird, three-dimensional dance. He stood on the edge of the airfield, alternately raising his field-glasses or shading his eyes with his hands as he watched the practising pilots above. Even without identifying the serial numbers he thought he could pick out Joe and George — Joe flew with a fluency that none of the others could hope to share, while George handled his machine with a peculiar deliberation and economy of movement. Perowne considered himself lucky to have them both. He lifted the glasses again and swore softly to himself: one of the latest replacements had still to learn not to expose his belly — if he'd arrived six weeks ago, when the squadron was still in the south, he would've been dead within a day.

Training continued for another month with the days shortening rapidly as November opened and as the freezing winds swept over the fells. Perowne believed he had convinced himself that the younger pilots were improving. George constantly expressed his doubts: 'Two of them are reasonable — John and Alan. Jimmy Riley has the makings of a good pilot, but he'll try too hard to be a hero — he reminds me of Lex, with the same swagger about him. But young Gerry Barham should never have got this far. He'll never survive his first dogfight — and he'll probably kill someone else in the process.'

The pilots spent more hours on the ground, discussing

tactics, with Perowne chalking formations on the board and trying to breath reality into the flat diagrams. No words could express the confusion which surrounded aerial combat. He decided the squadron should develop still further the tactical lessons learnt from grim experience during the year: at the time of Dunkirk and the battle for France formations had been too inflexible, with the aircraft flying close together and the pilots therefore having to keep as close a watch on each other as they had for sight of the enemy. Perowne had loosened the V soon afterwards, also allocating a rear-guard to fly slightly above and behind. This seemed to work: surprise attacks were reduced. Then Perowne noticed that the rear-guard himself was vulnerable. Increasingly he detailed a more experienced pilot for such a role, with this aircraft flying in a weaving fashion.

Further changes now seemed necessary. One had already come about through force of circumstances. To begin with each section had comprised the maximum number of aircraft available, taking into account the fact that some pilots should, if possible, remain on the ground to act as a second string. Sections were therefore anything up to six or seven aircraft. Gradually the numbers dropped through the reduction in the total squadron strength, sometimes down to as few as three per section but more often five machines. Lately the section total had worked out at four, and Perowne noticed the benefits which this even number brought. Four aircraft patrolling in rough V-formation gave an unequal number to one side, and this extra man could act as the weaving rear-guard. Above all, four men could automatically move into two pairs once combat began. One man guarded the other; groupings of odd numbers of aircraft, on the other hand, meant someone being left out and becoming a sitting duck in the combat area.

Perowne now formalised his sections into four aircraft comprising two pairs. This would give him three sections, led by himself, George and Joe. As far as possible the sections would always consist of the same men; likewise the pairing within the section would remain the same, although Perowne realized this amounted to a vain hope – in all probability the pilots would be coming and going far too quickly.

George approved the arrangement, and took a detailed part in the discussions; as always, his attitude remained that of a chess-player. Joe also agreed, but Perowne guessed that he disliked the idea of becoming a section leader and the responsibility for the lives of other men which the role carried.

Training continued, both on the ground and in the air when weather permitted, and with the training went the waiting. It seemed to Perowne that an air of expectancy hung over the squadron. Around the airfield were the preparations for intensified war: the scrubland surrounding Catterick swarmed with soldiers engaged on constant manoeuvres; tanks whined and screeched over the gorse; regiments were being reorganised and rearmed, switching from their defensive role. The winter minimized chances of a German invasion, and it seemed that the troops were being moved from the beaches prior to taking the offensive. Perowne and the other pilots tried to guess where that offensive might be, but even George failed to come up with a satisfactory answer. Only North Africa provided an active overseas theatre, and news from this front remained hazy apart from first reports of a push by Wavell's Western Desert Force against the Italians, apparently highly successful.

So the uncertainty continued. All the more unreal after the events of the last year. Previous months had been so definite: each pilot knew his immediate purpose, even though he could only see a day ahead not knowing if he would survive more than twenty-four hours. Now the horizon had been lifted. But the future was blurred, although no less ominous.

FIVE

One more respite was allowed to the squadron before being thrown back into the whirlpool of war. Permission reached Perowne in mid-December for the pilots to have six days of leave over Christmas; each man responded to the news in his own fashion — Shaw and Lawson planned a detailed pub-crawl of the nearby Newcastle area; Osborne would go with his wife to his in-laws at Stoke; Henny intended to enjoy himself in London; the youngsters — Phil, John, Alan, Jimmy and Gerry — would go home. George told no one of his plans.

Perowne and Joe decided to celebrate in a foursome with Anna and Susie. Perowne suggested the idea and at first Joe hesitated: his friend was also his CO, the 'old man', and although they had an easy relationship while at work, he felt apprehensive over the contact between them away from the station. The five years' difference might begin to gape. And Joe hadn't seen Anna since that moment when she'd smiled into his eyes and bent forward to kiss him, his hand on her breast.

'What's the matter?' asked Perowne. 'Don't you want to share your Lakes with us?' So Joe agreed to book in at a Langdale hotel. Yet a fresh doubt arose. He wanted to be with Susie, and his longing for her company had risen sharply; her letters were warm and affectionate, loving in her quiet way. But he still didn't know how to treat her. Feelings which had grown between them during the perilous summer were still unspoken; Joe had yet to touch her in any other way than a gentle caress. He told himself that this was because of her youth, but he knew another reason existed. He didn't want to destroy the freshness which surrounded her, in just the same way that a picked wild flower so soon faded.

Now Joe stood by the telephone outside the officers' mess, preparing to ring the hotel, and not knowing what to say when he booked the rooms, and wondering what Susie's reaction would be if she were asked to share the same bedroom with him. Then Joe suddenly smiled. 'I'm acting like a kid,' he said to himself — but when he spoke to the woman at the hotel he nevertheless asked for two singles, and a double for Anna and Teddy.

Anna and Susie travelled up together; Teddy and Joe motored over to Kendal in a borrowed battered car and met them at the station. The girls walked down the almost deserted platform, and Joe wanted to walk forward but hesitated with Teddy standing there beside him. Anna turned smiling to Joe after hugging Teddy and her lips lightly brushed his cheek. Susie made no move to kiss him, and Joe's shyness still held him back; instead they simply stood holding both hands.

They drove north from Kendal, this time with Joe at the wheel, and headed over the Lakeland foothills to Windermere and then to the end of the lake and up the curving road into Langdale. Anna and Teddy sat in the back, arms tight around each other; Susie sat next to Joe, listening to the excitement in his voice as he described the views around them. Through the roadside pines Susie could see the glimmer of small lakes; behind loomed the mountains, pressing into the narrow valley, their lower slopes coated with red bracken which ended abruptly at the tumbling grey stone screes. Clouds hung heavy over the summits, but down in the valley the evening sun reflected the blue on the barn slates and the rich greens of the tiny walled fields. It seemed a world away from the gentle curves of the Kentish countryside, and Susie felt apprehensive at the overpowering strength of it all. Night began to creep faster down the fellsides and the blackness thickened in the pines.

Oil-lamps were already glowing in the small hotel. A

huge fire crackled in the granite hearth, and the four of them sat to eat a massive ham and egg tea; then Anna sat on the floor between Teddy and Joe, each elbow on one of their knees, and Susie sat on the floor beside her, face turned towards the flames.

'Now,' said Anna. 'Let's have a pact.'

'What on earth are you talking about?' asked Perowne.

'No talk of the war, from any of us. Let's forget it. We'll just walk and natter and be ourselves. But first I know what I'm going to do.' She stood, reaching for Teddy. 'I'm going to bed.— and you're coming too.'

He pretended to resist. 'Who says you'll forget about the war. If I hadn't been away these last weeks you wouldn't be dragging me to bed so soon.'

'Don't you believe it.' Anna's hand rested on Joe's shoulder as she passed his chair, and he could feel the gentle pressure of her fingers. 'Goodnight you two.'

Joe's shyness returned as he sat with Susie. She remained sitting on the floor, knees beneath her chin, with the glow from the fire reflecting on her face. She suddenly said: 'I like Anna. Do you?'

'Of course – and Teddy.'

'He reminds me of you a bit. Gentle. She's very beautiful.' Susie suddenly turned to him, smiling. 'Thank you for asking me to come. Peter was very jealous.'

For the next four days they disregarded the weather even though it rained in chilling, sudden bursts, and they walked further into the surrounding mountains; they returned each evening to hot baths and huge meals after which they sat before the fire. For two evenings Anna sketched Susie, with Susie sitting on her cushion before the hearth. They gradually worked their way higher up the slopes with each walk, and the shared exertion brought them closer together. Anna and Joe never mentioned the night which the pilot had spent in the flat, yet the knowledge of what had passed between them provided an intimacy which gave pleasure to them both, heightened rather than lessened by their belief that such a revelation of emotion would never again be shared by them. The girls established a friendship which revealed a side to Susie that Joe had never really seen before – a teasing, laughing Susie full of chatter. 'Once she begins to talk she never stops,' laughed Anna. 'I can't get a word in – mind you I haven't breath for it anyway.'

On the fourth day they drove past Grasmere to the lower range of Helvellyn, then they climbed above Thirlmere through the pines and onto Helvellyn itself. They scrambled across the scree slopes and stopped to eat their packed food with the view stretching over the ranges to the west; they walked on, higher towards Helvellyn's hidden summit. The small sheep scuttled over the peaty hummocks; the crows flapped insolently across the mountainside. The ground steadily became steeper.

Joe led the way, Susie close behind him with a gap between them and the other two. Joe suddenly stopped, and Susie stood beside him. They'd reached the narrow summit ridge, and the stark contrast between the smooth slopes which they'd climbed and the harsh features on the other side of the summit frightened Susie: a few feet in front the ground dropped sheer, black rocks tumbling towards a small forlorn tarn and rising again on the far side in a granite precipice seemingly impossible to climb.

Susie reached for Joe's hand. Instead he put his arm round her shoulders and she moved closer against him with the fear still strong inside her. He said: 'It's almost like flying. I never tire of it.' To Susie it seemed strange that someone as gentle as Joe should love something so harsh; perhaps the very harshness had made him gentle. She slid from beneath his arm and walked slowly forward the few paces to the edge of the cliff, fighting down her fear: if Joe loved this place, then so must she.

Joe's eyes moved from the hills and peaks around him to the slight figure of the girl: the wind tugged her skirt against her hips, and the heavy walking shoes and thick socks served only to emphasise the slenderness and smooth curve of her calves; her hair tossed from beneath her scarf to curl around her cheeks. He desired her, up there on the mountain, more than ever before; he wanted to walk forward and put his arms around her to cup her breasts in his palms, and he wanted to press his loins against her. But Joe stood unmoving.

'Good heavens – I wouldn't stand on the edge like that.' Anna's voice sounded breathless as she reached the summit ridge. 'You're braver than I.' Susie turned, smiling gently, her eyes on Joe's face, and he found it impossible to guess whether she knew his thoughts.

They sat for a while in the shelter of the summit cairn, and Joe named the surrounding peaks and dales – Grisedale Pike, Chapel Crags, Kirkfell, Scafell rising higher. Then Joe pointed to a distant blue smudge of woodland which disappeared into a sharp, lonely valley.

'My father lives down there,' he said.

Teddy looked at him in surprise. 'I never knew we were so close.' Anna asked: 'Why don't we all visit him?'

Joe smiled. 'He wouldn't welcome us – he'd be friendly enough, but he doesn't much care for people. He's a vet, and prefers animals. I suppose most people would say he lives a lonely life, but he's happy, and I think I know what he means. We get on well.'

'Why don't you go?' asked Teddy.

'It doesn't work, not while I'm a pilot. It seems strange being there. I've tried it. I get the feeling while I'm there that he wants me to keep away until the war is over. I make him think of things that he wants to ignore, if he can.'

Next day was Christmas, and their last day at the hotel. They'd agreed to exchange no presents, not even between Teddy and Anna – 'we'll celebrate in other ways' she said to him. They walked in the morning and afternoon, and returned to an even bigger meal than usual and to a fire which licked high up the wide chimney. Outside the rain beat on the small, mullioned windows, and the black-out shutters seemed intended not to hide the oil-lamps from an unlikely enemy, but to increase the warmth and comfort of those secure inside the thick-walled building.

Anna sketched Susie again, refusing to allow her work to be seen since it remained unfinished. 'You'll have to come and stay with me in London, Susie, then I can do an oil. Promise?' Susie nodded. Then Anna and Teddy went to bed, their arms around each other as they climbed the narrow stairs. Joe and Susie sat silent for a moment, and Joe fought to keep his thoughts from the next day and the departure and the return to the squadron.

Susie rose from her cushion on the floor and came to him. She stood before him for a moment, and he looked up, but the glow of the flames behind her hid the expression on her face. She turned and settled on the floor between his open knees, and he didn't know whether the pressure of her head against his thigh resulted from innocence or a lover's invitation. He stroked her hair, almost shyly, and said: 'Someday soon we'll come again, you and I, and I'll take you to see my father. Will you come?' Susie reached up to take Joe's fingers; lightly she kissed his palm and then rested his hand against her cheek, and Joe could feel the warmth of the fire on her skin.

Kendal station had been transformed. Before, when Anna and Susie had arrived, there seemed to be no passengers for the trains. Now, when they departed, the platform was crammed with people. The men wore khaki or blue; heavy kitbags and knapsacks were piled beside the track; the flag-stones resounded with the scrape of boots; a dull smell of serge uniforms and rifle-oil mingled with the acrid fumes of soot and smoke from the waiting engine. All the soldiers, sailors and airmen seemed to have the faces of Cumberland and Westmorland farmers: the ruddy complexions, high cheek-bones, fair Nordic hair. With Christmas over they had filed from the fells and farms and were returning for another season of war.

SIX

Below Perowne the sea stretched like beaten pewter with patches glinting bright in the fitful January sun. Perowne glanced to right and left and checked his mirror; all three squadron sections were airborne, George leading Yellow Section to Perowne's starboard, Joe with the remaining aircraft to port. Ahead, a deeper grey line marked the approaching enemy coast.

The squadron had returned south ten days earlier. Since then one week had been spent in final training before Perowne's pilots became officially operational again. First duties had entailed providing cover for Channel shipping and patrols had been undertaken without incident; the enemy seemed comparatively inactive.

Now the squadron was taking the offensive. Orders included taking part in high-level sweeps and low-level strikes over occupied territory, code-named respectively 'circuses' and 'rhubarbs'. Today the target would be relatively short-ranged, allowing some opportunity for the pilots to work themselves in before penetrating deeper into enemy areas: Perowne banked slightly and looked below him – there, flying at about 20,000 feet, were the six Blenheim bombers which the squadron would cover for an attack on Dunkirk flak ships.

Perowne remembered the flights made along this route nine months before, when the squadron Spitfires had followed the huge smear across the sky originating from the blazing oil dumps at Dunkirk. At last the pilots were hitting back, even though on restricted scale. Perowne also recalled how, during the summer, it had been foolhardy to fly more than a mile or so from the safety of the English coast. Now the Channel had almost been crossed, and the details of Dunkirk were emerging rapidly, and the first flak bursts were beginning to pollute the sky ahead.

Perowne spoke over the R/T, and the Spitfires began to circle, guarding against intervention from enemy fighters. The Blenheims began an immediate bombing run over the shipping in Dunkirk harbour, and despite his preoccupation with watching for Messerschmitts, Perowne was unable to avoid observing the attack taking place below. Flak appeared so thick that it blackened entire areas of sky and the falling shrapnel sent up sheets of water, yet the six ponderous bombers continued to lumber forwards. The first three dropped their loads, huge sprouts of water erupting far beneath them; the second trio approached their targets. Suddenly one disappeared in an immense burst of flame: one moment the aircraft had been alive, the next it had completely disappeared.

'Jesus Christ!' Perowne recognized Osborne's voice.

'Hello Piper Leader.' This time George spoke. 'Bandits below to port. Looks as if they've just taken off. About six of them.'

'I see them.' The Messerschmitts were dim shapes moving rapidly over the dark green Belgian fields. 'OK Yellow and Blue Sections, go get them.' George and Joe immediately peeled away, their Spitfires diving in line astern behind them: eight against six, and attacking with the advantage of height – but of those eight Spitfire pilots, half had never been in combat before. Perowne watched from high above, still glancing for further enemy fighters yet equally anxious to witness the performance of his pilots far below.

Gerry Barham nipped his trembling lip between his teeth and tried not to look at the Messerschmitts rising to meet him. Instead he fixed his eyes firmly on the tail of Osborne's Spitfire, diving to his immediate front. Gerry had tried hard to prepare himself for this moment: he'd tried to imagine that the mock dogfights had been real. But he'd never imagined the utter dryness of his throat, the throbbing in his temples, the roaring in his ears. His aircraft felt too heavy for him to handle and it seemed to be weighing him down, taking him to inevitable destruction, and all the while those sinister shapes were reaching up to kill him.

Suddenly Gerry saw tracer ripping from the leading Spitfire as Osborne fired. At the same moment Gerry also jammed his thumb down on the button, automatically carrying out the same actions as the man in front; nothing happened, and even greater panic struck him until he realized he'd forgotten to slip off the safety catch – and dimly he also realized that if the guns had fired the unaimed bullets would have hit Osborne's aircraft. He fumbled with the catch, his shaking fingers clumsy in their thick gloves; Osborne was firing again, then suddenly he rolled to starboard to follow a wounded Messerschmitt, and the sky opened in front of Gerry.

Now he himself was leading the line of diving Spitfires. His wide, terrified eyes searched the path ahead. At first he could see nothing but the murky fields and dark woods below and he thought the enemy must have gone. Then he saw a point of yellow, growing larger, and on either side of this splash of colour were short dark lines, and he knew that the enemy fighter was coming directly up to meet him. Gerry jabbed his thumb down again, holding it there and sobbing as the bullets from his guns sprayed out in front of him; the Messerschmitt's yellow nose was becoming larger and still Gerry kept his thumb down on the button. Suddenly the yellow burst into red; the black lines on either side twirled violently as the wings started to spin, then they slowed and stuck like the hands of a clock. Gerry's guns ceased to fire; he sobbed even louder, pressing his thumb again and again not realizing that his ammunition had gone. The Messerschmitt was huge in

69

front of him, and Gerry's arms and legs seemed too weak to manoeuvre his Spitfire. But suddenly the flames leapt high from the enemy fighter and the machine tilted over onto its back, exposing its pale belly like a dying fish, and it slipped from Gerry's sight.

Somehow he found strength to pull back the stick. He began to rise, seeking escape, to climb as high as possible from the terrors beneath him, scarcely aware that he had killed and could claim a victory.

Perowne still circled, noting the results of the combat. He'd seen Gerry's triumph, and he smiled slightly with relief; he'd seen Jimmy Riley chasing a Messerschmitt, failing to find his target but flying with determination and considerable skill. Perowne had also noted the Messerschmitt torn to shreds by Joe and Henny, and the wounded enemy fighter which barely managed to escape from Osborne. All the Spitfires still flew. He spoke over the R/T, keeping his voice matter-of-fact in an effort to slow the racing pulses of the pilots. 'Well done Piper Squadron. A good first day. We'll join up and go home – the bomber boys are waiting.'

Gerry stood at the bar that evening surrounded by John, Jimmy and Alan. The youngsters were celebrating the victory; Gerry had become drunk very quickly, and now he leant against the bar with sweat shining on his freckled face, one arm hanging limp by his side and the other clutching a full glass of beer. Hazily, he doubted whether he'd be able to drink the pint before he had to rush outside. He tried to join in the singing around him but found it difficult to remember the words of the chorus, even though he'd sung this rugger song so many times at school the previous winter. The others kept slapping him on the back and telling him how great he was, but he still didn't really know why, yet at least the beer had swilled away his fear, for the moment. He couldn't remember how frightened he'd been; now, in his befuddled mind, it had all seemed so easy, and he couldn't really see why Jimmy should keep bleating in his ear about how jealous he felt. 'Why am I a lucky sod?' he slurred. 'You can do it tomorrow. Just go out and sodding well get one. Doesn't cost you anything.'

George, Henny and Osborne sat in the armchairs playing cards, occasionally glancing at the foursome by the bar.

'If they sing that blasted song again,' grunted Osborne, 'I'll ring their chicken necks.'

'Leave them be,' said Henny, shuffling the cards between his thin fingers. 'You used to be like that once.'

George commented quietly: 'It's easy enough to learn to kill – harder to learn how to stay alive.'

Osborne grimaced at the cards Henny tossed him. 'At least they're cheerful,' he said. 'It'll be different in the morning.'

The squadron flew for another week without loss. For three days foul weather prevented flying; the next morning all three sections took off but the bombers and fighters turned back after encountering heavy cloud near the French coast, and the pilots waited in vain during the afternoon for conditions to clear. Two sections, led by George and Joe, escorted Blenheims on a high bombing raid the following morning. They crossed the coast near Béthune flying at 28,000 feet and aiming for an industrial complex in the Chocques area; thick cloud still covered the French countryside, and Joe detected a group of 109s silhouetted against the white but George decided the Spitfires should stay with the bombers. Soon afterwards the clouds began to thin and finally cleared just before the target area; the bombs slanted downwards, and the return flight began. It proved uneventful. So too did another mission next day, this time a repeat attack on the Dunkirk flak vessels, although Osborne's engine began to misbehave while re-crossing the Channel and he landed with the Spitfire sounding like a monstrous motor-bike. Bad weather clamped down again for twenty-four hours, during which the squadron remained inactive except for a short escort role for Channel shipping.

Events seemed to be standing still. Officially the squadron had adopted an offensive role, yet Perowne now realized how limited this would be. Even the bombing attacks seemed strangely negative, with no definable results apart from the sight of the smoke and the haphazard explosions far below. Meanwhile the lack of activity caused tension to rise amongst the pilots: the older members of the squadron were able to shoulder the burden of waiting, but the younger pilots were showing signs of stretched nerves: Gerry and John were even more quiet than usual, whereas Jimmy reacted in opposite fashion, becoming increasingly vocal in his demand for an opportunity to fight.

Suddenly the clouds lifted, leaving the sky a pale, cold blue. The January sunshine even contained a false hint of spring; the day promised to be busy. All three sections took off at 10.15, immediately joining with a Hurricane squadron from the neighbouring airfield, and the fighters flew to their rendezvous with bombers for another raid on the Béthune area.

The Hurricane and Spitfire cover climbed to just over 32,000 feet – the highest Perowne had yet flown. He'd warned his pilots to prepare for the cold, but the extent of the temperature drop still surprised him. His fingers were especially painful, with the freezing metal of the control column striking through the thick outer gloves and then through the inner silk; he found some relief from easing back his fingers inside the cloth so that they weren't jammed into the glove tips, but still the ache spread up his arms, making his limbs heavy. The pain seemed to be affecting his mind, and he believed for a moment that he must be suffering from the effects of the oxygen; he shook

72

his head in an attempt to clear it and concentrated on his instruments and on the positioning of his pilots.

They crossed the French coast still flying at a height of over 32,000 feet, and the land far below appeared as a section of a gigantic globe, curving away into the haze to east and west. The bomber pilots began to talk over the R/T as they readied themselves for their runs over the target – this time a weapons factory.

Then the bomber squadron leader suddenly spoke to Perowne. 'Hello Piper Leader. Bandits. Bandits. Please engage.' Perowne acknowledged and led his three sections in a steep dive, leaving the Hurricanes to continue the high-level escort.

Joe saw the enemy first. 'Here they come Piper Leader. A dozen or more to port climbing fast. And more coming up behind.'

'I see them. Follow me in.' Perowne pressed the rudder bar, forgetting his numbed feet, and rolled to the left. The sections fell in their prearranged pattern, each section splitting into pairs, and within twenty seconds the dogfights had erupted above Béthune. Perowne's fire lacerated one enemy machine; he spared no time to see if the 109 had been destroyed but switched his attention to another trying to reach the bombers. Osborne, acting as his Number Two, reported: 'The Blenheims are going in'; the 109 jigged in Perowne's sights, dived in avoiding action, and Perowne flung his Spitfire in a similar movement; the fighter rose in his sights again, drifted behind the projected yellow light on the windscreen, and Perowne's guns began to clatter. He glimpsed an aircraft falling from the sky to his right and noted the machine to be a Spitfire, then Osborne yelled: 'On your tail Teddy. Dive!' Perowne kicked the rudder bar to twirl his Spitfire onto its back, then yanked the stick hard into his stomach, and his aircraft dropped vertically. He levelled at about 5,000 feet to see a Messerschmitt just below him; in front of the enemy a Spitfire weaved and twisted in an attempt to escape. Perowne noted Henny's number as he dived in pursuit.

The three aircraft dropped lower, until Perowne's altimeter registered 1,000 feet. The gap between his Spitfire and the Messerschmitt was closing fast, but suddenly he noticed smoke beginning to blow back from Henny's machine. The wounded aircraft twisted with increasing desperation, sinking still further towards the fields. Perowne fired a two second burst at Henny's pursuer, then another, and his second attempt caught the Messerschmitt. The enemy machine jumped into a near vertical position, nose down, then slammed directly into the earth.

Perowne spoke over the R/T. 'OK Henny, he's gone. You can take it easy now.'

'Thanks Teddy. But my Spit's no go.'

'Can't you gain height?'

'No.'

'Then bale out.'

'I think I'm too low. I'm going to try and bring her down. Switching off now. Good luck, Teddy.'

Perowne climbed slightly, cut his speed, and watched Henny gliding down to land. He'd chosen a stubble field, yellow with a faint tinge of green, stretching long and straight beside a row of poplars. On the other side of the poplars ran a road. And only when Henny's machine had almost touched its racing shadow on the field did Perowne notice the trucks and the troops.

'Henny! Huns – on the road!'

Henny had switched off his R/T. Perowne banked to keep him in sight; the Spitfire was taxiing across the grass, smoke pouring thicker from the tail, and already Perowne could see the German soldiers jumping from their vehicles and climbing the fence into the field. And Perowne also saw another Spitfire, with Jimmy's number, streaking in below him. Fire from Jimmy's guns was kicking up the earth in a line reaching towards the Germans.

'Jimmy! For Christ's sake leave them alone!'

Perowne's tight circle continued. Jimmy's bullets stitched onwards, passing the Germans; Perowne saw Henny, standing in his cockpit with his arms raised, and the sudden way in which the pilot toppled forward onto the wing when the Germans opened fire.

'You bloody fool Jimmy – they might've let him live.' Jimmy still failed to answer; instead his Spitfire banked for another strafing run, and this time Perowne dived to follow him. They flew just above the height of the poplars. Perowne kept his thumb tight on the button; he felt the blast of an explosion as his bullets hit one of the trucks and ahead of him the scything machine-gun fire cut down the men as they crouched exposed on the open road. He began to climb again to make for the Channel, and he felt strangely sickened, since this was the first time he'd ever killed other than fellow airmen.

Back home, Perowne learnt that Phil Brookes had died – Phil, always so fragile: it seemed to Perowne that the boy had already outlived his life. His Spitfire had failed to pull out of a dive. John had also gone, although no one had seen him and he might now be a prisoner. So, with Henny, the squadron had lost three pilots. Perowne, standing in the bar, noticed the effect on the others – George and Osborne were playing cards, as they had been with Henny the previous evening, and they made no mention of him in their conversation; Shaw and Lawson joined their game and soon their cheerful bantering filled one corner of the room. Alan, Gerry and Jimmy sat on their stools by the bar, silent. Jimmy apologised to Perowne: 'I swear I didn't hear you tell me not to shoot at those Huns. I must have left my R/T on transmit, Sir.' Perowne let the subject drop and bought the three boys a drink – perhaps the Germans would have shot Henny anyway, provoked or not.

Joe sat in the farmhouse kitchen. 'I'm not sure whether

75

we're any better than the Germans,' he said. 'On those bombing raids I mean.'

Peter looked across the table at him, puzzled. Joe continued: 'We fly across there and the Blenheims just drop their loads – what's the difference between that and the German raids on London?'

'Heavens above – there's all the difference.'

'You tell me.'

'Well, they started it didn't they? And you're not attacking women and children. You're killing Germans, and a damn good thing.'

'Are we? Those people down there are French – men, women and kids. A bomber at 25,000 feet or so can't aim. It just blasts the whole area. We might kill a few Germans – but how many French people get slaughtered in the process?'

Peter stood up impatiently. 'Well, you don't press the button anyway.' Then he grinned. 'Soon I'll be flying – and I know damn well I won't have a conscience. Come on, let's go down to the pub for a beer.'

Susie watched them leave the kitchen. Only a few weeks before Joe had looked so healthy and fit; since then his skin had become paler, and the dark circles had reappeared beneath his eyes. He'd never mentioned the Lakes again, or his home, or his promise to take her to see his father.

Soon Peter would also be gone – Peter, so young, who considered it to be an adventure, who looked upon Joe as a hero even though barely two years separated them in age. Susie had always been so close to her twin brother, but his attitude to the war and to the prospect of fighting had pushed them apart. Yet in one way they'd been drawn closer than ever, through their feelings for Joe. Joe linked them together. But the link seemed increasingly frail: Joe could go at any moment.

SEVEN

The squadron flew one more mission over France, without loss, before bad weather once again restricted operations. Each day the pilots waited for the clouds to lift and the increase in tension accelerated. Singing dwindled in the mess; most nights the bar was almost empty. Perowne's anxiety grew rapidly together with his desire for action: a few successes might lift the squadron's lethargy. Another replacement arrived, immediately nicknamed Button through the shape of his nose: his Spitfire flying hours were totally inadequate. Another feature gave Perowne increasing concern: the squadron had somehow become cold, lacking the intimacy of former days. Then, at the time of the summer battles, everyone had been thrown together; it seemed easy to know what was going on – if a pilot baled out, he could telephone the mess and joke with the others about his mishap, or he might walk into Dispersal later in the day, ready to fight again. The pilots seemed to belong to each other.

Now this had changed. The squadron role seemed ineffectual, both through the weather and the nature of the attacks themselves, with no means of assessing the results of the bombing. Moreover, men died in a strange country, or simply disappeared too easily with no one able to guess their fate. And the survivors were becoming split into groups: George, Joe, Osborne and Perowne himself in one group, Shaw and Lawson in one of their own, and the four youngsters in the third. Contact between them was difficult, especially between the first and the third. The older pilots had known the previous intimacy, which seemed gone for good. However much he tried, Perowne felt estranged from the young, and he knew George, Joe and Osborne felt the same.

Yet they all had to fight together and depended upon one another, and Perowne began to fear that this might be impossible. Men who found it difficult to talk together in the mess would find it increasingly hard to achieve almost instinctive coordination in the heat of battle. Perowne could think of no solution. He needed someone like Simon, with his easy good humour and companionship, to help weld them all together. But Simon was gone, rejected and embittered – unless ... Perowne reached across his desk and pulled a pad of paper towards him, and he began to write.

A week later two letters reached the farmhouse, one for Peter and the other for Susie, the first in a large brown envelope, the second covered with an untidy and almost indecipherable scrawl. Peter ripped his open. 'I know what it is. Yes – look!' The letter contained official confirmation that Peter would begin his basic air training in two weeks time, providing final medical tests proved satisfactory.

Susie spread her letter on the table and tried to read the writing. Simon's signature ended the brief note. 'I need your help. I've badgered them into giving me another medical, and they've agreed – I think Teddy Perowne has been doing a bit of pestering. I'm bloody sure they'll pass me. But I'm scared Susie. The medical is in London and I've got to go on Friday afternoon. Could you come with me Susie? I can't think of anyone else. It's the people in the streets – I'm not sure I can stand being seen. Would you meet me? I wouldn't mind them looking if you were with me. I could believe they were just looking at you. Please meet me Susie. I know you will.'

Susie passed the letter to Peter. He skimmed it through then looked up, grinning. 'Good old Simon – I knew he'd bully his way in the end.' Susie took the breakfast plates to the sink; soon Peter would be gone, she thought, and the fears which she felt for Joe would

78

be duplicated with her brother, and now Simon was asking her for help in his effort to kill again. Susie felt as if a great pressure were weighing her down. But she wiped her hands on her apron and simply said: 'I'll ring the hospital now.'

The wind blew wet and blustery early on the Friday morning, and the streets were still streaming with rain when Susie reached London in the early afternoon. People ran from doorway to doorway, heads down, and the wind rattled the protective sheeting over the shop windows. Susie entered Waterloo station to wait for Simon. The platforms were crowded with passengers waiting for the irregular trains: bombs had damaged some lines the previous night and these were still being repaired. Susie stood beneath the station clock and read the sombre newspaper placards: 'German pressure on Yugoslavia – Greece threatened.'

Around Susie people were bustling to find trains, saying goodbyes, trying to find taxis, queueing for buses, servicemen with tin hats tied to their packs, civilians in drab economy clothing. Susie wished she were back at the farm. Simon's train was late and she wandered round the station, increasingly depressed. She returned to the clock. Then she saw him limping slowly through the crowd, the collar of his uniform coat turned up, hat pulled low, a scarf wound high round his neck. Susie walked quickly over and took his arm.

They walked slowly across Waterloo Bridge to the Aldwych and down the Strand, the rain still falling. On either side they passed bombed buildings, some with weeds already forcing through the rubble, others newly scarred; the streets seemed dirtier than they had been when Susie last visited London, with litter in the gutters and sand on the pavement spilled from the bags shielding the shops; advertising posters were ragged and torn, hanging sodden. They found a small, dingy cafe in a side-street off the Strand, and Simon sat in a dark corner while Susie fetched coffee and sandwiches. She sat opposite him, shivering as her wet skirt fell cold against her legs; her hair felt plastered stiff to her head.

'I'm sorry,' said Simon. 'You shouldn't have come. You must be drenched.' Then he added: 'God Susie, I'm so nervous. I've never been so scared. Those doctors petrify me.'

'You'll be fine.'

'With a face like mine you'd think they'd welcome me to frighten the Huns away.'

Fifty minutes remained until his appointment. They talked quietly, Susie sipping the weak, almost tasteless coffee; Simon pushed aside his sandwiches, too nervous to eat, and he constantly checked his watch. At last it was time to go. The rain had stopped and clouds scudded black over the grey sky; they walked to Charing Cross where they caught a bus to take them to the RAF medical centre in Chelsea. Simon gave Susie the money to buy the tickets and sat hunched against the window, staring through the steamed glass at the battered buildings as they moved slowly through the afternoon traffic down Whitehall and through Westminster.

They stood at the entrance to the tall grimy building; Susie, her hand through Simon's arm, could feel his body quivering. They arranged to meet later in a cafe round the corner, and she watched him as he climbed the steps and entered the blue-painted door: he dragged his right leg despite his effort to walk erect, and he kept his right hand – the one with three fingers missing – tucked deep into his greatcoat pocket; he didn't look back at her and the door swung decisively shut behind him.

Susie wandered through Sloane Square, where the plane trees stood leafless and apparently lifeless, blackened by the morning rain. Pale afternoon sun had begun to break between the ragged clouds over London, and Susie could see the moon already rising white and almost full. She walked to the cafe and sat at the window waiting for Simon; outside, the street started to darken.

The sun had almost set by the time Susie saw Simon walking along the pavement. His limp was more noticeable now, his foot slurring along the pavement slabs, and she knew he'd failed.

She helped him into a chair. He sat silent, then exclaimed: 'Christ – I want to get drunk.'

'We can have a drink if you like.'

'Then we bloody will.'

They went into the empty bar of a nearby pub. Simon ordered, his face averted; the barman barely glanced at him before returning to his stool and his newspaper at the far end of the counter.

'No chance. No chance they said. I'm never to fly.'

'Did they say why not?'

'They spouted a load of rubbish. Those bastards don't know a thing. Who are they to say if I can fly or not? They say my coordination isn't right or something, whatever that may mean, and that I couldn't possibly fly without all my fingers.' He mimicked an educated accent. 'I told them what to do with their bloody fingers and that I could fly with my teeth if I wanted to. They laughed. They laughed at me Susie and thought I was joking.'

'What will you do now?'

'Christ knows. They say I can have a squadron desk job – Intelligence, adjutant, control – something like that. I told them not to bother. I couldn't do it Susie. I couldn't sit on my backside and watch the boys taking off to fight.'

Susie allowed him to talk without interruption and she sipped her drink. He ordered another for himself.

'That's it then,' he said as he returned to the table. 'I might as well walk under a bus. A face which makes people retch. Can't live with myself. Can't bloody live – that's what it comes to.'

Simon had almost finished his third drink when the distant sirens began to wail. He appeared not to notice.

81

'Will you try again?'

'No. That's it. Finish.'

Nearby sirens had taken up the scream from those further east. Susie heard the faint thudding of bombs and the moan of aircraft high overhead, and then thin tinkling from the glass pearls of the bar chandelier as its chain started to shake. The barman folded his paper, stuffed it into his pocket, and called down the counter: 'Time for the shelter.'

Bombs were louder now, thundering towards them, and AA guns in the vicinity suddenly began to crash, and the chandelier bounced on the heavy chain. Susie helped Simon to his feet and hurried him through the door; she heard the barman close the catch behind them. At first the street seemed black. Then the houses opposite were suddenly silhouetted against a flashing sky. Susie and Simon stood in the porch, the sirens wailing insistently; further down the street a mass of people were hurrying into an underground shelter, and Susie began to lead Simon towards the crowd.

Bombs burst from the direction of Victoria. Susie could feel the pavement trembling; her dried throat hurt when she tried to swallow. Simon moved too slowly.

'Let's hurry Simon! I'll help you.'

She heard shouts and whistles; ahead of them the crowd was pushing and shoving into the narrow shelter entrance. She almost dragged Simon with her. The siren suddenly ceased to wail. And in the silence Susie heard the rising screech of a bomb and almost immediately it exploded behind them. Susie heard the sliding, crashing roar of falling masonry and felt hot air against the back of her head. Shrieks split from the crowd ahead, and then the whistling whine sounded again from above their heads.

Simon jerked, almost pulling Susie off her feet as he threw her into a doorway, his body shielding her from the street. The bomb landed barely a hundred yards away. It threw a massive roof upwards, and Susie watched horrified with her head pressed against Simon's shoulder as the side of the house toppled forward on the other side of the road: it fell slowly, evenly, then split in the centre and hurtled onwards to shower bricks and glass and huge steel girders. Someone on the pavement opposite had been thrown forward by the blast, and through the cloud of dust Susie watched the crumpled figure stir, rise and stagger towards the shelter. She attempted to move from the doorway but Simon's arms were gripped tight around her.

'We must get to the shelter,' she sobbed.

His voice was close to her ear. 'I can't.'

She turned her head quickly upwards to see his face lit by the flames of the burning house and fixed in the direction of the crowded doorway to the shelter.

'Simon! Come on!' She tried to tug herself free.

'Those people. Crammed in there. I can't. There's too many. I'll be crushed up to them, to their faces.'

'Please Simon. Please!'

'They'll see me.'

'We'll be killed!'

'Why the hell should I live?'

Susie heard another screaming bomb. She dropped to her knees and Simon crouched alongside, his body still as a shield, and she felt him suddenly thrust hard against her by the blast of the explosion; above his shoulder she saw the searing white glare, and she cried aloud from the noise in her ears. Then she wriggled between Simon and the side of the doorway, and half crawled across the pavement towards the shelter.

This time Susie didn't hear the dropping bomb. Nor did she even hear the explosion. Suddenly she was flattened against the pavement as if a huge hand had slapped her down. She lay with her cheek against the slabs and she could see them moving, rippling close to her face. She closed her eyes. She could feel the pebble necklace which Joe had given her pressed into her breast, and she wanted to remain there in peace. Instead she felt hands turning her and lifting. Simon cradled her in his arms and ran limping towards the shelter with glass crunching beneath his feet. He staggered down the steps sobbing for breath, and people crammed on the nearest bench shuffled even closer together to find them room; Simon placed Susie gently on the seat and sat beside her, her head to his chest and his hands smoothing her hair.

'I could've killed you. My God I could've killed you.'

'I'm all right.'

He tilted back her head. 'Are you sure?' She nodded. The sickly light from the bare bulb in the shelter ceiling made his face look even worse, heightening the vivid scars, and emphasising the absence of his nose because the remaining mound was insufficiently pronounced to cast a shadow. 'I'm all right,' she repeated. 'We're here now.'

Susie straightened away from him, leaning against the cold concrete wall. Her ears still rang from the noise of the bombs in the street. Other explosions sounded from outside, the nearest causing the dust to float thicker in the shelter, and the bulb swayed to flicker the shadows the length of the narrow room. People sat on benches stretching along each wall; others were squatting on the dirty floor; some had blankets and cushions. A baby cried incessantly. Nearby a group of men were playing cards, beer bottles beside them, and some women were busy knitting.

Suddenly Susie became aware of the fat woman sitting opposite staring, expressionless, at Simon. The woman nudged her neighbour and pointed, and Susie felt anger rising above the fear inside her. The two women didn't even shift their eyes when another bomb sent more dust sprinkling from the roof. They began to whisper, until the fat woman leant forward over the basket on her knees to tap Simon's knee.

84

'Pilot?'

Simon nodded. The woman sat back, smiling with satisfaction. 'Thought so. Here, have a sweetie.' She rummaged in her basket and found a grubby paper bag. 'Do you good. Gets away the taste of dust. Take two. Pre-war they are. Any teeth? Doesn't matter anyhow — you can suck 'em.'

Her neighbour, almost as plump as her friend, looked across at Susie. 'You're lucky dearie,' she said. 'He can't get any worse. Blimey, you should see my old man. Married him handsome didn't I and he's bleeding horrible now. Isn't he Doris? He's got a shiner the size of a marrow. Win a prize at Kew wouldn't it. Least your hubby can't get like that.'

The two women beamed across the narrow shelter, and Susie smiled back. 'Been married long?' asked the fat woman, and before Susie could answer she continued: 'Best thing — to get married. No good to wait. Have a bit of happiness I say. And you be proud of him, love. And watch him — he's still got a bit of sparkle in his eyes hasn't he? Bet he gets the girls going — don't you mate?'

Explosions stamped nearer again, increasingly determined, and Susie's fear surged upwards from her stomach. She suddenly wanted to stand and run — anything but sit trapped and helpless, waiting. The elderly man pressed next to her was trembling and Susie could see his fingers digging white into his knee; further down the shelter another child began whimpering. The baby still cried and the clicking of the women's knitting needles continued remorselessly against the background of the falling bombs; Susie clamped her teeth tight to stop herself screaming. She could imagine the bombs whistling through the black night sky towards the shelter, and she tried to keep her eyes from staring at the roof; Simon turned to her and she attempted to smile and his fingers found her hand, squeezing tight; she gripped him so hard in return that she knew she must be hurting him.

85

A man sitting near the shelter entrance suddenly whimpered aloud. He stood, still sobbing, a middle-aged man whose terror had torn through his respectability and self-control, and he started to scramble up the steps. Simon jumped up and ran towards him, grabbing the man round the waist and pulling him back into the shelter. Someone shouted: 'Let him go mate! It'll be his own bloody fault if he catches one.' Simon kept the man pressed hard against the concrete. He thrust his face close and shouted above the explosions: 'See this! Look at me! If you go out there you'll end looking so bloody horrible that I'll seem pretty – look at me damn you!'

The din quietened again. Simon eased his grip and allowed the man to slump down onto the bench, then he walked back to Susie apparently oblivious to all those looking at him. Susie rested her head on his shoulder, and there she stayed, trying to press her face deep enough into his rough coat to overcome the stifling shelter stench of dust, sweat and urine.

The streets reeked when the all-clear sounded and Susie stumbled outside. She was scarcely aware of the burning houses, the black pools of water, the hoses criss-crossing the pavements; dimly she remembered Simon taking her down King's Road and then into a side-street. They climbed stone steps and Simon rang the bell, with no response. They sat and waited, Simon's arm around her, until Anna came home.

Anna helped her undress, and started to take Joe's necklace from around her neck until Susie stopped her, whispering that she always wore it. Anna smiled. Susie's shivering gradually ceased. Then she sat wrapped in Anna's red housecoat, sipping hot chocolate, saying little and becoming conscious of her surroundings.

'Of course I'll take the job,' Simon was saying. 'I couldn't just do nothing – could I? Besides, I might end up in Teddy's squadron again if he pulls a few strings, and goodness knows he needs me.' Simon grinned. 'I can still teach them a thing or two.'

Susie slipped into Anna's bed. First she lay on her back, her eyes staring into the darkness above her, and then she turned towards the other girl. Anna said nothing; she merely put her arm round Susie's shoulder to hold her against the softness of her breast.

Perowne received the squadron orders three days later. He immediately called George and Joe into his office.

'I thought I'd tell you first. We're packing up here. We go back to Yorkshire, this time to Church Fenton – but not for long. We've just three weeks in which to switch from Spits to Hurricanes and get ourselves sorted out. And then we get an immediate overseas posting.'

Joe asked: 'Where to?'

'Goodness knows. It seems damn crazy to me. The squadron isn't in very good shape. We're two men short, Button has still to get his feet wet, Alan and Jimmy have still to score. We're all at sixes and sevens. It would be hard enough anyway, without changing machines and without flitting abroad.'

'I know where we're going,' said George. He pulled the morning newspaper from his tunic pocket. 'It's obvious.' He put the newspaper down on the desk, the headlines facing Perowne who read: 'Churchill warns Hitler – Hands Off the Balkans'. And in smaller type: 'Greece prepares for Nazi invasion.'

EIGHT

Joe crawled into the Hurricane's cockpit and adjusted the Sutton harness around him, fastening the straps loosely so that he could lean forward to fight off blackouts. He revved the Merlin engine, holding the brakes on. Then he attached the oxygen tube to the tank and plugged the radio cord to the R/T set, checked the instruments, and he gently eased the brakes. The Hurricane began to roll forward, like a monster whose leash had been slipped and yet who couldn't quite believe his freedom.

The aircraft gathered speed with each invisible revolution of the three-blade propeller. Joe checked again to see that the field remained clear, flipped the magneto switches to test them, then adjusted the variable-pitch propeller at full fine and set the carburettor boost. He kept the engine only about two-thirds open for the take-off, and the ground dropped steadily beneath him changing from the green of the Yorkshire airfield to the lusher grass of the surrounding pastures. Joe boosted the aircraft into a steep angled climb.

Already, after three days at Church Fenton, Joe felt at ease with his new aircraft. He relished the strength of the Hurricane Two, with the Merlin 22 engine developing 1,460 horse-power, and above all he enjoyed the machine's manoeuvrability. At first, like the other pilots, he'd been cautious of the new creature, but within a day had learnt to throw the aircraft into tight direction changes by using the wide-open throttle and thrusting the stick almost into the corners of the cockpit.

Now, just over nine minutes from take-off, Joe reached 18,000 feet. Waiting for him was Gerry Barham; Joe flicked his R/T to transmit. 'OK Yellow

Three, let's go.' The two aircraft began to twirl in a mock dogfight, sometimes rising to 25,000 feet, sometimes dipping low. And while he flew, Joe thought that Perowne had been correct — Gerry was still far from being proficient, and, according to Teddy, the same applied to Alan and Button. Jimmy Riley seemed more skilled, if he could curb his eagerness, and the latest arrival Dickie appeared competent — perhaps because he'd moved directly from training aircraft to Hurricanes.

Joe shot Gerry down for the third time. 'Christ, Yellow Three,' he said over the R/T, 'you exposed your belly again when you banked and rolled. Come in for another pass.'

Four minutes later Joe spoke again. 'Gerry — I circled down behind you then. If an aircraft comes at your rear like that don't climb — he'll just continue his arc and shoot you to hell. Roll and dive instead.' And later: 'Loosen up Gerry. Forget about flying your crate. Just concentrate on fighting. That comes first.'

Day by day the training continued. Perowne tried to convince himself that the squadron was ready to fight, but he knew that at least a third of the pilots were unprepared for battle. Another replacement reached the squadron and this pilot, Arthur Tatham, brought with him experience gained from his previous posting with another Hurricane outfit — he'd been fighting since early September, based at Tangmere, and his operational experience matched that of Osborne. But it seemed to Perowne that the newcomer might take time to adapt to his new home: he resented leaving his old squadron.

Less than a fortnight remained before the scheduled departure overseas. Perowne had still to be told officially of the squadron's destination, but it seemed almost certain that George had been correct and soon they would be fighting in Greece. Perowne anxiously studied the available news from the Balkans and disliked what he read: newspapers reported a steady build-up of German infantry and Panzer divisions in south Germany, Hungary, Romania and Bulgaria, all encircling Yugoslavia's land frontier and with the forces in Bulgaria also threatening northern Greece. Fighting between Greeks and Italians in Albania intensified in the second half of February, and although the newspapers declared that the Greeks were holding their own, the lack of Italian success was believed to have enraged Hitler still further. Churchill was quoted as saying: 'Britain will honour her commitments to Greece.'

The telephone suddenly jangled on Perowne's desk. He recognized the other voice immediately. 'Simon! What're you up to?'

'You wangled it Teddy. I'm coming back to you.'

'Thank God for that.'

'An official telegram is on the way, but I thought I'd be the first to tell you. I'll be your Field Intelligence Officer, whatever that might mean.'

'We need you Simon, whatever you're called.'

Suddenly training ended and Perowne could do no more. The twelve pilots and the mechanics and the remainder of the ground staff dispersed for their forty-eight hours of leave. Perowne took the train to London, to Anna, and also to meet Simon. Joe drove him to the station. 'Give Anna my love,' said Joe. 'Tell her we'll look after the Old Man.' Perowne answered: 'And give Susie mine. I might've known you'd lure her up here again.'

Susie arrived on the next train. Then the small open car bounced over the stationyard cobbles and out onto the road which led to the Lakes, and to Joe's home. Susie snuggled down in the seat, hair tucked in and collar high under her ears, and after a mile or so Joe reached out to take her hand.

They approached the cottage just before dark. Snow reflected the fading light on the peaks above the narrow valley, reaching down towards the screes and the black, mysterious pine forests. The car tyres crackled over the frosty surface of the rutted road, and Susie shivered as the cold air struck her beneath the trees.

'I hope he's got something ready for us,' said Joe.

'Does he mind you coming?'

'Not once I told him I was bringing you. He can pretend I'm just taking a girl home to show him, rather than coming on my last leave.'

Joe slowed the car and turned the vehicle into a narrow track, running upwards between the pines. He drove for another twenty yards then stopped. 'We have to walk now. I've a spare pair of boots for you in the back — probably too big, but they'll do. It's not far.'

He held her hand as they walked, her suitcase in the other and his haversack on his back. The thin track rose steadily, a black ribbon against the frosty white grass on either side; the pines dropped beneath them. They clambered over a wall, and Susie smelt the sweet odour of sheep; suddenly the track dropped again into a tree-lined dip and a light shone ahead. They crossed a small paddock and the white walls of the cottage rose before them in the murk, the oil lamp beckoning through the small window beside the door. A dog barked and the door swung open as they entered the cobbled back yard.

The large, broad-shouldered man stood outlined against the light, silent for a moment. Joe ceased to walk forward and allowed Susie's hand to fall. Then the man suddenly bellowed: 'Joe! Come in with you.' He flung out his arms and grasped them round Joe's shoulders when the boy hurried forward. 'Why did you come in uniform boy? It stinks of war.' 'It's clean today.' 'I tell you it stinks.' He called again, one arm still around Joe.

'Come on then girl, into the warm. Let's see what Joe's been jabbering about these last months.'

Joe's father seemed even bigger in the small, crowded room. His grey hair hung thick and ragged; his clothes were baggy, clearly thrown on for comfort without thought to appearance. As he looked at Susie she saw that his eyes were Joe's — dark, sensitive, smiling. He reached out to embrace her in the same way that he'd done with his son, and when the rough tweed of his jacket pressed against her cheek she could smell the moors and the pines. She noticed his hands were also Joe's, with the same long and delicate fingers.

'Aye, you'll do,' he said. 'You must be famished — I've a good stew in the pot.'

Later they sat in front of the fire. Susie looked about her: the room was crammed with books; boots were piled on the flagstones behind the door, beneath the coats tossed on the pegs.

'Do you see many people?' she asked.

'No — nor fancy it. Only farmers when I mend their animals. I don't want more. You can keep the rest. This is what it's all about.' He leant forward and touched Susie's knee. 'This is where it all begins — with God's creatures. Not that I'm religious, not in the churchy sense. But those that mistreat a creature, no matter how small, find it that much easier to mistreat their own kind. I want none of it. Nor does Joe, if the truth be told. He should be here with me.'

'I haven't much choice.'

'Happen not. But it's where you belong. Pray God you'll be back before long.' He turned to Susie again. 'And what about you lass?'

'Me?'

'Aye, thee. Would you be lonely in a spot like this?'

Susie shook her head, smiling at them both. 'I'd feel at home,' she answered.

They walked slowly up through the pines. The weather had warmed overnight and streams around them gurgled with melted snow, racing and bouncing over the stones to the swollen beck below.

'There'll be a massive carpet of bluebells up here soon,' said Joe. 'If you half-close your eyes it looks like the sky turned upside down. And the primroses will be out in another month.'

They would return south in another day. They suddenly halted, both turning to the other. Joe's hands slowly lifted to hold Susie's neck lightly beneath her fair hair; her arms reached round his waist, and she raised her head. The pine needles were soft and thick beneath their feet. Joe moved his hands to frame her face, the long strands of hair falling softly over his fingers, and slowly he bent to kiss her. Their lips met gently, barely more than a faint touch, and they drew apart for another moment still close enough for him to feel her rapid breath on his skin. Then they came together again this time with a growing strength; he felt her hands pressing him close and her lips opening beneath his own. He moved his hands lower to the small of her back and then to her hips, and he brought her loins to the hardness of his own.

Joe eased himself gently away, still with his arms around her. Susie's lips were still apart, wet and waiting for him again; her blue eyes revealed her readiness for his body. He imagined the nakedness of her beneath the trees, her warm body against the soft cold carpet, the smell of her skin mingling with the crushed pine needles beneath her.

'No Susie,' he whispered. 'Not yet. It would be too much like a goodbye.'

Gently she kissed him once more. 'Then we'll wait.' She smiled. 'We'll come here again. There'll be plenty of time.'

He unbuttoned the top of her blouse and pulled out

the pebble necklace; he kissed the stone, warmed from its resting place between her breasts, and he held it in his fingers for a moment before gently replacing it. 'Keep it warm for me,' he said.

Perowne, George, Joe and Simon sat together in the crowded stinking aircraft. Only by shouting could they hear themselves speak above the noise of the engines; chinks in the fuselage permitted razor-edged draughts to pierce the hold in which they crouched. The Liberator's bomb-racks had been removed, but the space was filled with men and equipment, and blankets on the ribbed iron floor offered the only comfort. Perowne's watch had stopped, probably broken by the vibrations and by the sudden jolts in the air pockets, and he tried to calculate the time and even the day. They'd left Lyneham just before midnight, 2 April, flying low over the Wiltshire countryside until they reached the coast in order to be recognized by British batteries; they'd reached Gibraltar during the morning of the 3rd. The aircraft had taken off again at 6 p.m. the same day, arriving at Malta in the early hours of the 4th after a dangerous flight through Nazi air space in the western Mediterranean. They'd stayed on the island for the rest of the day and for much of that night, leaving three hours or so before dawn. Perowne therefore reckoned it to be 5 April, about 7 a.m.

Joe slept beside him, his head rolling against his chest; Simon snored next in the line, the noise of his breathing accentuated by the lack of his nose, and Perowne wondered if he would ever get used to the sight of the mutilated face; George sat with elbows on his knees, awake although with his eyes closed.

Cramp struck Perowne's right calf; he scrambled to his feet, clutching the side of the curved hull for support, and he eased the aching muscle. At the same moment the noise of the Liberator's engine changed pitch.

94

Perowne clambered forward over the bodies of the RAF personnel littering the hold, and he climbed the short ladder into the cockpit; already the aircraft's squat nose had begun to drop. Perowne stood behind the pilot looking at the vista ahead.

The sky seemed an even more startling blue after the drabness of the British winter and after the gloom of the Liberator's hold. No clouds smudged the wash of colour. The sea appeared almost mauve, deepening to purple in the distance. And there, along the entire shimmering horizon with the details emerging from the pale ochre background, rose the Peloponnese and the islands of threatened Greece.

NINE

Air Commodore d'Albiac, commanding the RAF in Greece, stood before the map sheets which had been pasted together to provide coverage from the Pindus mountains northwards to the Albanian and Bulgarian borders. Perowne sat with Simon and other officers on the wooden benches. Eight hours had passed since the Liberator had landed; during that time Perowne had flown north from Athens to the squadron airfield near Ioannina, where he had been dismayed by the totally inadequate facilities and by the state of the Hurricanes issued to the pilots. Simon had immediately commented: 'Christ, I'm glad they won't let me fly.' Maintenance equipment was almost non-existent; the squadron was to be housed in a makeshift tent encampment; the take-off area comprised a muddy field beside Ioannina lake, extremely exposed and with protection only comprising one anti-aircraft battery. And half of Perowne's pilots, including Osborne, Shaw and Lawson, had still to arrive after their Liberator had been delayed by an air raid on Malta. Perowne had barely time to fling his baggage in his tent and issue initial orders before he had to fly westwards over the mountains to the plain of Thessaly and to d'Albiac's open-air briefing at RAF GHQ outside Larissa. Now Simon, acting as Intelligence Officer, was busy scribbling notes as the Air Commodore spoke.

'I know your difficulties gentlemen. No one sympathises more than I. But I'll speak frankly. Many of you have come from the Western Desert, where things have been going damn well. We want them to continue to do so. The Italians have been pushed back almost to El Agheila. We've advanced 500 miles in two months. But

96

supply difficulties are increasing. And the Germans must be considering sending substantial help. We can't take any more aircraft or equipment from the desert. Others of you have just come from home. And things are in pretty short supply there too.'

D'Albiac turned towards the map. 'So we have to make do with what we've got, and that's precious little. General Maitland Wilson's staff will explain the military dispositions in detail, but I'll give you the broad picture as it is today. As many of you know, the main Greek lines are in this area.' His stick pointed north to the region east of the Struma river, close to the Bulgarian border. 'We had hoped they would deploy further back, in the Aliakmon line south of Salonika, giving greater time for preparations and better defence in depth, but they preferred to stay near the frontier. General Maitland Wilson's units are moving northwards to position themselves in support at these main points.' D'Albiac indicated just to the south of the Greek defences. 'Enemy forces in Bulgaria lie south of the Moritza river, comprising the 12th Army under List, with the headquarters in Sophia. Air reconnaisance reveals considerable movement towards the frontier.'

The Air Commodore turned back to his audience. 'Gentlemen, we're heavily outnumbered. I won't give you precise figures, but there is the danger that the German forces will overwhelm the initial Greek positions near the Bulgarian border, no matter how valiantly the Greeks fight. Our troops, a 4-division force of just 57,000 men, have still to settle in the required positions. An assault on the Bulgarian front may well coincide with renewed pressure on the Greeks in Albania. Moreover, it is probable that the Germans moving from Bulgaria will attempt to encircle the Greeks by aiming to thrust round behind, with Salonika the main objective. In this case the main weight may well fall on the British Expeditionary Force now moving northwards.'

D'Albiac paused for a moment. 'The RAF will be called upon to provide maximum support. Our strength amounts to the equivalent of eight fighter and bomber squadrons – roughly 80 serviceable aircraft. Of these, there are only about 30 serviceable fighters. Luftwaffe total aircraft strength is likely to be in the region of 300 machines. So, as far as fighters are concerned, we must expect a ratio of at least ten to one – with no prospects of reinforcements.'

Perowne listened while the RAF commander detailed the duties to be undertaken and the tactics to be followed – the bombing missions for the Blenheims, the strafing and ground support roles for the Hurricanes and anti-quated Gladiator biplanes. Technical officers provided information on call-signs, communications networks, refuelling facilities. The evening sun slanted golden over the mountains to the north, striking the faces of the assembled squadron leaders; Perowne felt uncomfortable in his thick uniform – he'd had no time to find himself summer service clothing.

An hour later Perowne and Simon flew back over the ranges in the battered Anson transport which had been placed at the Squadron's disposal. Below them the mountain clefts lay in night shadow while the setting sun still fired the peaks. The squadron airfield was shrouded in almost total darkness when the Anson turned in to land, with the moon shimmering on the nearby lake; improvised lights flared fitfully from kerosene cans, and the Anson's wheels lurched blindly over the ruts in the grass. By the time the twin propellors had ceased to whirl, Greeks were already running to douse the kerosene flames with sodden sacks, and the smell of the snuffed fires caught in Perowne's nostrils as he stumbled towards the tents.

Chaos still surrounded the squadron. Mechanics were trying to tinker with Hurricane engines aided only by the light from small torches; men struggled to locate equipment and tools in the dark, cursing and damning the useless situation in which they found themselves. Perowne immediately called his pilots into his tent. They crowded in, their faces already tired from the uncomfortable flight, their skin pallid from the chill English climate; Perowne studied them as they entered — Button and Dickie, neither of whom had yet fired a shot in combat, then Arthur Tatham, Joe and George coming last. Perowne asked George if any news had been received of the remaining six pilots still on their way from Malta. 'They should be arriving late tomorrow,' replied George, 'weather and Huns permitting.'

Simon used his notes to brief the pilots on the detailed situation; then Perowne spoke. 'It couldn't be much worse. But at least we can find some consolation in that — we're starting from the bottom and can only go up. With any luck we may have a week or so to get ourselves straightened out, and a week could make all the difference.'

Early next morning, 6 April, before the sun had time to surface from the dark Aegean Sea, the Panzers began screeching forward along the narrow mountain roads from Bulgaria, and the lorries crammed with German infantry filed in long convoys behind them, and the Luftwaffe droned south to blast the fragile Greek defences. Perowne received first reports from Larissa, with the radio crackling and whining from the interference caused by the mountains. Within six minutes Perowne was airborne, leading his five available pilots, instructed to intercept Luftwaffe bombing raids north of Salonika.

The Hurricanes rose into the dawn. The sun pierced up to them from the plain of Thessaly, turning the machines to glowing pink and hiding for a moment the scars of their hulls. Over the R/T came a cacophony of voices — English, Greek and sometimes German and Italian — as the mountain currents distorted frequencies, and Perowne found it difficult to distinguish one frenzied message from another. His section soared and fell in the air pockets seemingly detached from the battle chaos further north.

They reached the Greeks' positions during an interval between bombing raids and were immediately diverted closer to the Bulgarian frontier to undertake strafing runs on the advancing Germans. Only a few miles separated the two lines. The Hurricanes sank to 5,000 feet above the scrubby yellow fields and olive-grove blotches, and within two minutes Perowne noted the dust rising from an approaching German convoy. He issued his instructions: the five aircraft behind him slipped into line astern, with the line snaking suddenly low.

Perowne closed on the convoy less than 150 feet above the stony road. He glimpsed a tank amongst the olives, then a second. Another Panzer still moved in the centre of the road, squat and with its gun traversed to the right. Perowne began to fire: his bullets swept over the tank and over a following lorry; he altered course slightly to aim along the edge of the road where men were crouching, and he saw the flailing arms as his bullets cut a path before him. The road bent, causing Perowne to overshoot, and he banked hard to port. As he did so he noticed the other Hurricanes flying low behind him, but with one missing.

The remaining four followed Perowne's curve, and he led them in again. Smoke now billowed from the convoy, and he could see the bodies and crawling wounded men as he flew above: one man staggered in the centre of the road, hands clutching his lowered head, but Perowne's bullets cut him down. Yet when Perowne reached the head of the convoy he saw the tanks already moving: the advance had hardly been hindered.

Perowne noted his fuel situation and received instructions to put down at a Greek airfield in the Salonika suburbs. His pilots formed formation on either side of him; he checked the numbers and found the missing machine belonged to Arthur Tatham. No one had seen him go, although George had noticed him slipping behind as they made their strafing approach.

Black raw craters were punched in the yellow earth of the Salonika airfield. The Hurricanes manoeuvred their way in, one behind the other, and two tankers were already moving out from the perimeter buildings. Perowne slid open his canopy and the warm air rushed in to disperse the smell of his sweat.

'Don't be with us long, Sir.' The Greek mechanic standing on the Hurricane's wing was looking down at him. 'The *Germanoi* soon visit us again.' The mechanic grinned and rubbed his curly black hair with oily fingers. 'They come all the time. *Boum Boum.*'

The Hurricanes roared aloft heading for the battlefield which crept towards them, and the day dissolved into a blur of wavering vehicles and running men and streaming tracer, all revolving round the sun.

Arthur Tatham had pulled away after his engine began to die. He'd managed to gain sufficient height to glide along the valley of the Aliakmon, but decided to land in a terraced field near Karperon, knowing he would never make it over the high mountain spine to Ioannina. He reached the squadron late that night, riding in the cabin of a delapidated truck whose windscreen was almost obliterated by crucifixes and flowers, and he staggered amongst the tents, reeling from the effects of retsina, insisting on drinking a final toast with his equally drunk Greek friends.

The other six pilots had still to arrive from Malta. 'Christ knows where they are,' said Simon. 'I reckon they've done a bunk and gone home again.' News from the fighting had deteriorated throughout the day with German pressure north of Salonika becoming increas-

101

ingly intense, and there were already signs that the Greek positions were beginning to bend. 'They should pull back while they still can,' commented George, studying the map in Perowne's tent. 'Those damn Greeks are too proud. They don't want to lose land yet they can't see they're likely to lose the lot.' Other reports caused Perowne equal concern: evidence was accumulating of probable Italian efforts to push further forward against the Greeks on the Albanian front, and this area lay dangerously close to the squadron base at Ioannina. The airfield might soon come under heavy air attack. Already, RAF stations in the Larissa and Salonika region had suffered severe damage.

Joe shared a small tent with George and Simon. George, in his usual efficient fashion, had already worked out a solution to the problem of lack of space. 'There isn't room in those dratted things for more than one person to move around at the same time. So we'll have a rota system for going to bed, one going after the other.' Simon, sprawled on his campbed with a beer, grinned up at him. 'Just how organized can we get? It's OK by me – just as long as I'm last.'

Now Joe lay on his sagging bed, the blanket pulled around him against the chill night air. He could hear the clanks and scrapes as mechanics struggled to fix the Hurricanes in time for the morning. He thought of the German Panzers, continuing their relentless grind from the north, and in the distance he could hear gunfire, rumbling over the black mountains like summer thunder. Joe felt cold, and over-tired, and his mind reeled in reaction to the chaos of the day. He'd never hated war before: instead his emotions had been anticipation, fear rising to terror, then an almost calm acceptance; war had simply been there. Now it had been given an even deeper dimension. It seemed to hold greater menace: before, he had fought man for man in the sky and he could consider his enemy to be an individual, a person like himself, perhaps with similar feelings; now the enemy comprised a moving mass, and no matter how many men he slaughtered with his machine guns, others rose up to take their place and the deathly momentum would continue in an impersonal and gigantic wall of destruction.

Dickie followed George with the distance leaping shorter between the Hurricanes and the black shapes of the convoy ahead. The two aircraft banked round the terraced slope and levelled above the road; Dickie glimpsed sheep scurrying up the hillside, but his eyes remained on the vehicles in front of him. He smiled slightly. It seemed so easy; strafing was in his words 'a piece of cake'. He could forget the possibility of small arms fire from the ground, and could concentrate on killing. Now he straightened the Hurricane's wings, sat forward, selected the right-hand side of the road simply because last time he had chosen the left, and he pressed the button; his smile increased as the fabric on the Hurricane's wings fluttered with the vibration of the Brownings and as men below began to crumple. In some ways he felt detached from the destruction: his victims died silently, jerking and twisting like crazy puppets; in other respects he felt like the puppet-master pulling the strings. Too soon, the tail of the convoy fell beneath him as the Hurricanes began to rise.

'OK Yellow Section. Save the rest of the ammunition for the flight home.' George's voice sounded irritatingly calm compared with the exhilaration which Dickie still felt. But his excitement faded as the Hurricanes climbed above the hills. The smoke of Salonika mushroomed to the east; ahead stretched the sky which the Luftwaffe increasingly controlled.

The five Messerschmitts dropped from the sun. George had been expecting them, almost certain of their presence, and he experienced a sense of satisfaction when he detected the dots in the glare knowing his intuition had been correct. 'Bandits Yellow Section. Coming from the sun. We'll go up to meet them.'

Dickie glanced about him anxiously as he boosted his throttle to follow the section leader. To his left he noticed that Joe had almost drawn level, with Arthur flying directly behind him. Dickie squinted into the sun again, to see the distance rapidly narrowing between the two pairs of Hurricanes and the diving enemy. Fear filtered cold through his body and he began to shiver, yet at the same time his ungloved hands sweated on the stick. Fear turned to terror. Within seconds he would be fighting a death duel with a man probably superior to himself, and Dickie's feeling of hopeless inadequacy brought an almost unbearable desire to push forward the stick in an attempt to escape. Yet even in his terror he knew such an attempt would be futile and instead the sun scorched into his face, searing his eyes.

A black shape cut the glare. It seemed to Dickie that the Messerschmitt must be on fire, so strong did the sun burn behind it. Blindly he pressed the button. Almost immediately the bullets died, with too few left after his wanton firing at the convoy. The Hurricane began to shudder at almost the same moment that the wings ceased to vibrate from the useless guns; the control column leapt into life, jumping and jerking in Dickie's slippery hands. The glare of the sun blazed into the cockpit again, until the perspex became obliterated by spreading oil. The invisible nose of the Hurricane flicked towards earth, and the wings twisted to port revolving faster and faster and flinging Dickie against his harness. He still clutched the stick, his thumb on the firing button.

'Bale out Dickie! Bale out now.' George's voice sounded wonderfully close. Dickie forced himself to relinquish the hold on the control column; he unbuckled his harness, whimpering as his sweaty fingers fumbled with the catch, and then he slid back the canopy. Air sucked his breath from his body and below him the earth

104

spun in a tremendous arc of moving mountains; he tried to climb from his seat, only to find his right foot caught beneath the buckled rudder bar. Dickie tugged, the wind snatching at his chest. His shoe dropped from his foot and clattered against the side of the cockpit, but his ankle remained fast. Now the earth filled his twisting vision; his vomit sprayed; his Hurricane took him to death.

George circled above the explosion on the hillside. He banked one more time; goats, which had run in panic from the crashing aircraft, were huddled beneath the olive trees, and one or two had already begun to graze again amidst the bright spring flowers. George pulled back the stick, checked his position on the map, and headed south-west along the lonely winding valley.

Arthur had also died, his Hurricane shattered by a direct hit from a German 88mm gun as he flew low over a convoy, with his death coming before he had time to consider the squadron at home. Joe, leading his section, told Perowne that the exploding Hurricane probably caused more German casualties than all their machine gun fire.

The other pilots had at last arrived. Three – Osborne, Shaw, Lawson – were already airborne after an urgent request for help had been received from Greek foward troops south-east of Edessa. Perowne, sitting for the moment in the sun with Joe and George, therefore counted his strength as ten pilots; he felt greater concern from the unsatisfactory state of the Hurricanes. The majority suffered from oil leaks, and all were in obvious need of major overhaul.

Simon walked from the tent which he used as an office. He squatted beside Perowne and flapped a sheaf of papers on the ground in front of him. 'Details of the latest ground situation. Don't read them unless you want nightmares. The Greeks are getting plastered.'

The Greek line contracted still further during the night

— the second night since the German onslaught began. Next day brought constant calls for help: Perowne led one section up in the morning and another in the afternoon; George took his section up twice in the morning, twice more after a snatched lunch of fried corned beef; Joe returned with his four aircraft after darkness, completing his third mission of the day. The hours had passed in a whirlwind of strafing, dogfights, strikes against bombers; the clothes of the pilots were stiff with sweat, their arms and thighs ached; they slumped on their beds and immediately fell into drugged sleep, only to be roused within the hour by the barking of the anti-aircraft battery. Two bombs burst harmlessly on the hillside above the airfield, serving as warning for further raids to come.

It seemed almost miraculous to Perowne that none of his pilots had been killed or injured during the day. But tiredness and inexperience were beginning to tell: after the return from his last mission George had berated Gerry for flying too close, and the youngster had barely been able to keep back his tears when Perowne interrupted George's tirade. And two aircraft were unusable: Shaw had had to make a forced landing south of Salonika and was still absent — with Lawson's face pale with anxiety until he learnt his friend was safe; Button had written off his machine after making an atrocious landing during the late afternoon.

And the next day promised to be even more frenzied. Simon informed Perowne that intelligence reports revealed a steady stiffening of German pressure on the Greeks in Albania, with this front now only about fifty miles north-west of the airfield; Greek lines were shortening on the Salonika front, and the Germans seemed to be attempting a drive between these two regions, down through the central mountains to threaten the Greek left flank at Salonika. General Wilson, commanding the British forces, had moved the 1st Armoured Brigade to join an Australian brigade group to block this German thrust, and these troops were frantically attempting to dig in around Monastir in the mountains. Four of the missions undertaken by Perowne's pilots during the day had been against the Germans to the north of Monastir, but Perowne himself witnessed the rapidity of the enemy advance: in the short interval between his first and second flights the leading German units shifted ten miles further forward along the narrow winding roads.

Perowne bent beneath the open flap of his tent and stood to smell the early morning air. Light had just filtered through the passes to the east while cloud still hung on the ranges to the west. Perowne heard Simon cursing as he tried to shave his scarred face; in the distance the bells hanging round the necks of goats pasturing above Ioannina tinkled. A Hurricane engine roared into life, and then another followed by a third, and Joe's section began to move down the airfield on the squadron's first mission.

Then, as Perowne watched the Hurricanes, his eyes glimpsed a black dot moving immediately above Jimmy Riley's aircraft. The speck curved down, becoming almost invisible as it dropped beneath the skyline, but another replaced the first and then two more, and the first shape grew rapidly more distinct as it levelled towards the airfield.

'Messerschmitts!' Perowne shouted above the noise of the taxiing Hurricanes and began to run along the length of the tents. 'For Christ's sake – Messerschmitts! Get the hell out of there!'

The staccato stutter of machine guns pierced the noise of the Hurricanes' engines. Perowne glanced over his shoulder and threw himself flat as the enemy aircraft swept above him; bullets ripped into the tent to his right and immediately the canvas sagged and sank. From his left swept a blast of hot air and a huge roar, and Perowne

107

half-raised himself from the dirt to see Gerry Barham's Hurricane disintegrate in a mass of flame. The Messerschmitts banked for their second approach. Perowne ran towards the other Hurricanes parked beneath the trees beside the airfield; he saw Simon, hobbling in front of him on the same mission, and already George and Lawson were clambering into the machines. Simon fell, cursing as he struggled to his feet again, his face still half-covered with shaving soap; Perowne sprinted past him; the Messerschmitt machine guns began to clatter again.

Even before he glimpsed the Messerschmitt, Joe had seen the bullets kicking the soil towards him as he taxied for the take-off. His reactions were immediate; he swerved his Hurricane to starboard and the bullets flicked to his port less than six feet from the tip of the Hurricane's wing, and at the same time Joe boosted his speed to the limit. His wheels had just left the soil when the second Messerschmitt dived. Joe saw the narrow shape curving beyond the end of the airfield, flashes already spitting from the wings, and he thrust his aircraft further to starboard knowing he risked catching his wing-tip on the ground, then he pulled the stick even deeper into the pit of his stomach in his effort to climb. His Hurricane gained height, engine screaming in protest, with Joe already glancing around him for the enemy. He glimpsed the burning mass which had been Gerry's aircraft and below him he saw Jimmy Riley, seeking height like himself; yellow smoke spiralled from the tents, and beyond a black Messerschmitt cross streaked over the grey-blue lake towards the airfield. Joe checked his mirror, saw no threat from the rear, and immediately dived.

The Messerschmitt banked over the shore of the lake. Perowne could see the machine approaching as he flung himself into the cockpit of the parked Hurricane; the aircraft roared into life and began to roll forward, and at that moment the Messerschmitt's bullets raked a stationary Hurricane behind Perowne. The blast of the exploding machine buffeted his own aircraft, slewing round the tail; the starboard wheel leg collapsed, dropping the wing to the earth in a jolting, jarring lurch which threw Perowne against the side of the cockpit. Another eruption struck his tilting machine, causing the ruin to rock violently; Perowne crawled from the cockpit, vaguely seeing Joe's Hurricane flash above his head.

Joe fired a long burst, four seconds or more. His bullets fell beneath the target and the distance between the two aircraft was already rapidly increasing. Then another Hurricane dived above Joe's head, its shadow making him flinch and flick into a half-roll fearing an enemy attack; instead Jimmy Riley roared beyond him, using the speed of his sharper diving angle to pounce on the Messerschmitt. Joe straightened his aircraft in time to see Jimmy's bullets strike home, tearing away half the Messerschmitt's port wing; the enemy aircraft veered to starboard then slid downwards towards the lake, striking the surface of the water with a massive sheet of spray and bouncing once before disappearing. Joe banked away searching for another raider to engage, but the enemy had gone and he tightened his turn to come in to land.

Three mechanics had died in the explosions amongst the parked Hurricanes; three aircraft had been destroyed; Gerry's death brought pilot strength to nine, and the squadron had only 11 serviceable aircraft.

And within two hours the raiders returned. By now two squadron sections were aloft, one operating in the Salonika area, the other north of Monastir; of the remaining three aircraft on the ground, one received substantial damage to the rear fuselage. Mechanics were still working desperately on the damaged tail-plane when the Messerschmitts returned once more — one man was killed as he ran for cover, and this time the Hurricane burst into vivid orange and yellow flames. Perowne had stayed on the ground while the other eight pilots flew in the section missions, and now he resumed his telephone attempt to gain replacement machines. 'Can't help you old boy,' replied the harassed officer at Larissa, his voice faint on the line. 'All airfields have caught a packet, as far south as Athens. And it's going to get worse.'

'He's damn right it is,' commented Simon. 'HQ have just been on the radio. The Germans have reached Monastir. The blasted front is cracking open.'

One by one the pilots returned from their fourth sortie of the day. Each told of German columns pushing through the passes in the Monastir region and of German convoys thrown over the Struma river closing on Salonika. George flung his helmet and revolver on the table beside Perowne. 'The Greeks at Salonika will be lucky if they live another two-three days. They're getting hammered from the front and the Germans at Monastir can start rolling them up from the west.' British troops under Wilson still had their main deployment slightly further south, but Simon's information revealed that outlying elements had already suffered heavy casualties, especially in the Monastir region – and soon the British might be without Greek support. 'I spoke to a Major on Wilson's staff,' said Simon. 'He said it was all hell up there. They'd never time to settle in before the Huns attacked, and the Greeks were much too far forward – they got themselves stuck out on a limb and now that limb is being chopped off.'

Reports continued to reach Simon and Perowne during the night, some of them scrappy and garbled, others providing a reasonably reliable and clear picture of troop movements. From the messages and signals it emerged that leading German columns had begun to swerve south-east from Monastir, apparently pushing down the road which led to Florina. The road divided at this small mountain town, one route heading directly west for Salonika, the other winding over the ranges to Grevena and then to Ioannina. The squadron's airfield might soon be overrun.

Messerschmitts thundered over the airfield in the half-light next morning. Perowne had tried to spread his Hurricanes as widely as possible round the airfield perimeter, but protection remained virtually non-existent. Fire from the single anti-aircraft battery proved ineffectual. One more Hurricane was destroyed; the squadron now had nine aircraft for the nine pilots.

Sixty minutes later Perowne received orders from Larissa to evacuate his airfield: enemy forces were pushing too close, air attacks were likely to intensify, and Perowne's pilots must therefore move further south to Arta as soon as possible. According to the officer at the RAF GHQ: 'Please have your squadron operating in minimum time, and by early afternoon at the latest. Leave all unnecessary equipment behind.'

The weary pilots learnt the latest news as they returned from their section operations; Hurricanes were immediately refuelled and meanwhile the pilots crammed their belongings into haversacks, throwing them into the Anson, and they ate a hurried meal standing at the edge of the field. Even as the aircraft began to move down the take-off path again, trucks were pulling onto the dusty road with the remainder of the squadron personnel; Perowne circled once and already the airfield seemed to have a deserted and defeated appearance. Retreat had begun, and as George commented: 'It's probably started too damn late.'

111

Deep in the purple shade lay the German convoy. Joe banked his aircraft close to the valley side, his wings parallel to the slope; beneath him the road wound sharply into the gorge, disappearing into the shadows cast by the setting sun, and the last enemy vehicle had slipped from sight. Joe checked his fuel once more and noted the failing needle, and again felt tempted to turn for home. But beyond the gorge lay New Zealand troops desperately attempting to defend the road to Salonika, and the Germans in the pass would be able to strike during the difficult hours of night, unless delayed.

Joe switched his R/T and spoke to the other two Hurricanes. 'OK Blue Section. We'll follow the road. I'm going down.' He pushed his left foot on the rudder and moved the stick to level the aircraft, and he began his descent glancing over his shoulder to see Jimmy and Alan banking behind him. He flexed his fingers, settled into his seat; ahead, the entrance to the gorge seemed scarcely wider than his wings.

Sun struck the cockpit one last time. The cold shadow into which the Hurricane now roared spread even darker in contrast; the steep rocks on one side of the chasm reached above the aircraft in a black and almost overhanging wall, whilst the tips of those to port were still splashed with dazzling light. One hundred feet below Joe the grey road twisted, with a river tumbling white beside it. Joe thrust his foot on the rudder bar and banked his aircraft round a bend in the chasm, to see the last German lorry full in his sights. He fired immediately, still banking, but his bullets streaked beyond the target. Another truck moved ahead, and Joe's fire ripped through the canvas; he dropped even lower, to fifty feet, and his bullets caught the files of men scattering for cover amongst the boulders. An armoured car burst into flame; a lorry careered off the road and into the river.

Another bend in the gorge loomed ahead: Joe swerved his aircraft to starboard and the tip of his wing seemed to brush the rock. He struggled to level and his bullets sprayed the convoy again. His fire reached the leading vehicles; flames suddenly licked upwards, then Joe's Hurricane reached the open sky beyond and he climbed towards the sun.

Jimmy Riley followed Joe. He watched the section leader disappear into the gorge and turned to follow determined to forget the enemy and simply to concentrate on the task of flying. He knew himself to be an excellent pilot: the old man had said he was 'shaping up to being another Joe'. If Joe could do it, then so could he, and Jimmy experienced almost exhilaration at the challenge, with the chance to rival Joe's flying skill driving away fear. Jimmy therefore entered the gorge believing that the chasm acted as a greater enemy than the Germans, and confident that he would emerge as victor.

He flew superbly, following the line of the road round the first bend, his thin face bent forward, deep-set eyes fierce with determination. He levelled along the road, dimly conscious of burning vehicles below him, saving his concentration for the twisting route along which he had to fly. The second, sharper, bend rapidly approached, and for a moment he felt a surge of apprehension since the shadows hid the exit, and then the gap slid into his view, his feet and hands reacted accordingly, and the aircraft tilted to match the slope of the mountain.

Only now, with the sight of the open country, did the convoy become paramount in Jimmy's mind. He became aware of his thumb close to the firing button,

113

and he supposed he must have fired during his flight, but he couldn't remember when and he certainly hadn't selected a target. But Jimmy still smiled with satisfaction as he climbed to join Joe, believing he had proved himself an equal as a pilot.

Alan's loneliness swept over him when Joe then Jimmy disappeared, with his feeling of isolation combined with surging dread. Beyond that narrow entrance lay the chasm walls and the German guns, and Alan knew that if he survived the one he'd never escape the other. It was easy for Joe. Alan believed that his section leader had never felt fear: the youngster's attitude to the other pilot resembled the relationship experienced only the previous year between himself and the Head of his House at school — a feeling of hero-worship strengthened by the conviction that a great gap lay between them. With Jimmy it was different: Jimmy was his friend, and yet at the same time seemed to be like the fourth-form teenager who played for the first fifteen. And now Joe and Jimmy had left him, and he must follow.

Alan approached the entrance, and the walls seemed to close in upon him. Almost at the last moment his nerves failed; he suddenly wrenched the stick across the cockpit, slamming down his foot, and the Hurricane banked into the open again. It would be so easy to fly above the mountain; nor could he see that the lack of his contribution to the attack on the convoy would make any difference.

'Hello Blue Three.' Alan almost sobbed at the sound of Joe's voice. 'Come on Alan — it's not so bad. Doesn't take a minute, then it's all over.'

Alan hunched his slight body into the seat, his chin close to his chest, his elbows tight into his sides; he banked towards the chasm again, and his Hurricane wings seemed to grow larger at a far faster rate than the entrance amidst the rocks. He plunged into the shadow,

114

and felt as if blindfolded by the black, until the solid mountain wall rose before him. Frantically he banked, almost too far; he managed to correct the angle of the machine, only to twist the Hurricane again as the chasm continued to unravel around him. Orange flame flickered and flared from the darkness below; he remembered to press his thumb on the button, then jerked the stick to alter his course; the belly of the Hurricane seemed to be brushing the slope, and instinctively he winced as the boulders heaved below him; he pulled back the stick to escape, with the aircraft roaring across the width of the chasm at a crazy, impossible angle. Somehow he levelled, and even fired again; his aircraft rose slightly, and the sun seared into the cockpit, and he knew that if he continued to climb he would be safe. Instead he dived again, and his vision was split by yellow sunlight and black beams of shadow and tiny points of orange flame from the German guns. His aircraft screamed low for the final twist, with the weight of the machine dragging Alan's trembling arms, and with the orange dots suddenly exploding to fill his sight until the fire consumed his eyes.

Joe circled above the chasm exit. He saw Alan's aircraft bounce against the hillside and slither and twist into the open as a spitting, flaming globule, leaving a trail of burning wreckage and smoking scrub, and at last coming to rest beside the road to Salonika.

'OK Jimmy,' said Joe over the R/T. 'We can't do anymore. We'll go home.' Smoke from the burning German vehicles and the remains of the Hurricane rose together in the evening sky behind them.

Clouds thickened over the mountains soon after the squadron's arrival at the Arta airfield, rapidly becoming darker and heavier with rain, and thunder mingled with the rumble of distant artillery. Rain fell suddenly, sending the mechanics scrambling for cover beneath the aircraft wings, and pounding the canvas on the tents. Water soon filled the tyre ruts in the airfield and began to seep into the doorways of the tents, and the small stream behind the Operations Room suddenly roared into a torrent.

This Operations Room utilized the only solid structure on the improvised airfield, a plain stone building which still smelled of the goats which it had recently housed. A table had been placed in the centre, upon which were spread a large-scale map of the immediate area and another of the battlefield further north. Simon's table stood nearby, littered with papers. Around the room were strewn parachutes and Mae Wests, and helmets and revolvers hung from nails driven into the walls. Across the far end of the square building stood a rough dining table made from planks and boxes.

Now the pilots sat at this table, waiting for the telephone on Simon's desk to ring and for another operation to begin. The instrument remained silent. George put down his book, commenting: 'Thank God for the storm. It might keep the Huns quiet and give us a rest.' Perowne, sitting beside him, looked at the pilots lolling on their chairs: eight remained from the twelve who had arrived in Greece – George, Joe, Osborne, Shaw, Lawson, Button, Jimmy and himself; the squadron had been in Greece exactly one week. Of the survivors, Button showed signs of most strain; Simon had been attempting to cheer him up with stories of his stay in hospital, including the afternoon when his girl friend had gone to the wrong bed – his face had been swathed in bandages, and she'd failed to recognize him and had gone to another man equally covered with dressings, and Simon, unable to talk, was obliged to lay fuming whilst the other patient received her ministrations. These, and other tales, had succeeded in lifting the depression slightly, but now Button sat revolving his empty mug on the rough table, his eyes rimmed with red

116

as they stared at the planks in front of him; only he and Jimmy remained of the youngsters. Jimmy appeared to be thriving, although Perowne wondered how long the boy's brittle excitement would stay intact. Shaw and Lawson seemed as cheerful as ever; Osborne grumbled, but this was normal – as was Joe's quiet, withdrawn nature; George acted in his normal inscrutable and self-contained fashion.

Bright red playing cards lay scattered at one end of the table. Osborne collected them together, and Shaw and Lawson shifted their chairs to join him in a game. Meanwhile the rain drummed even heavier on the rusty tin roof. George lifted his eyes to the ceiling for a moment and murmured: 'It's difficult to tell whether the Gods are being kind or angry.'

'What the hell are you talking about?' asked Osborne.

'The Gods – they live in the mountains. Any good Greek will tell you. They've sent the rain to keep the Huns away. But the Germans will use the time to bring up more strength.'

Simon received a succession of reports on the fighting situation, and Perowne and George joined him at the map table in the attempt to sort some clear picture from the scrappy information. George found it easiest to cut his way through the confusion. British troops were managing to block the German approach from Monastir, helped by the foul weather which kept the Luftwaffe grounded. But German pressure on the sector close to the Albanian border had been maintained, and the possibility still existed that enemy forces would be able to thrust between the Greeks in the west and east, isolating both in turn. It appeared that only the British divisions under Maitland Wilson could keep the link between the two fronts, and that even if the Monastir thrust remained blocked, the British position might be eroded by a move from Albania further south – in

117

which case the British would themselves risk being surrounded.

Darkness fell unnaturally early with the mountains still obscured by thunder clouds. The noise of the rain on the canvas roofs of the tents continued into the night, and blankets were damp to the touch. Joe lay in the dark, listening to the sound of Simon's snoring and George's steady breathing; the absence of activity during the afternoon had heightened his anticipation for renewed fighting, probably tomorrow. He still felt no real fear, but as the numbers of pilots steadily dwindled he increasingly wondered, almost without emotion, when his turn would come. It must surely be soon.

Button also lay awake. The drumming of the rain beat into his head and he found it impossible to cut out the noise. He knew he would soon die. He faced this fact not with acceptance but with a terror which widened his eyes as they stared into the dark and which constricted his throat so tight that even his sobs were strangled. He imagined the various acts of death, one of which would be selected for him: his aircraft rushing towards the ground, the soil rising to crush him; flames eating his body; dropping through the sky, twisting and twirling after his parachute had failed to open – was it true that a falling man lost consciousness before hitting the ground, or would he feel the impact in that split second before death? Button remembered the various deaths which had been inflicted on the squadron – Alan's, Arthur's, Dickie's – and he envied these victims because for them it was all over; his terror arose not through the knowledge of death itself, but from the pain which he might have to endure in those last seconds of life.

Black clouds lightened to grey during the morning, but still the rain swept down from the dark mountains. Mud oozed over the shoes of the pilots as they hurried from their tents to the Ops Room and from the shelter of the building to check their waiting Hurricanes. The rain had washed the machines clean, and their long noses pointed upwards as if smelling the freshened air, but their wheels were sunk into the sodden earth, half hiding the tyres and making them seem reluctant to release their hold on the ground.

The first break in the clouds appeared to the west in the mid-afternoon. Within ten minutes calls for help were being received from the north: the Luftwaffe had resumed their bombing and strafing attacks. The Hurricanes were dragged and pushed onto firmer ground, and the first section laboured across the field and into the air; the second section left four minutes later.

Perowne led the initial flight, with Osborne his Number Two, and Shaw and Lawson making up the rest of the section. First they flew north-west, after receiving an urgent appeal from elements of the 12th Greek Division in the Salonika area: they arrived to find the attacking Dorniers gone and the Greek lines shrouded in smoke. Perowne took his section eastwards, towards Monastir, and on the way the Hurricanes encountered a Dornier formation escorted by Messerschmitts. Dogfights continued for five minutes: Perowne and Osborne converged on one bomber, destroying the machine within seconds, and another slipped away into cloud with smoke streaming from the port wing. Perowne and his Number Two set out on their return over the mountains.

At about the same time the squadron's second section was heavily engaged with Messerschmitts above Kozani. The Hurricanes enjoyed the advantage of height since the enemy aircraft were climbing below them from a strafing run. George immediately dived, with Joe close to his tail and Button and Jimmy Riley following.

Jimmy's confidence remained strong. His knowledge of his ability had been confirmed by his flight through the gorge with Joe the previous day; he believed himself

119

a match for anything which a Messerschmitt pilot might offer. Now he eased himself in his seat, eyes upon the reflector sight, and he chose his victim. The Messerschmitt rose towards him, banking slightly to port with the sun glancing for a moment on the canopy, and Jimmy calculated deflection as he closed the gap between them. His Hurricane responded to his touch, the engine roared with healthy power, he had full belts of ammunition; he readied himself for the inevitable kill.

Suddenly the Messerschmitt dived. Jimmy's thin face smiled: if the two aircraft had turned into a dive simultaneously, the enemy might have gained an advantage, but now, with the Hurricane already descending, the enemy could never hope to outpace his pursuer. Jimmy swooped with his throttle boosted to full power. The Messerschmitt grew larger in his sights, twirling in a last effort to live, but by then Jimmy's thumb was on the button. One short burst was sufficient. The Messerschmitt spun viciously to port and then plunged into cloud, with the blaze of its flames shining bright through the shallow murk. Jimmy pulled back the column and glanced below: black smoke polluted the white clouds beneath him. He turned to go. He wondered how many enemy aircraft Joe had shot down, and how soon he would overtake Joe's total, and as usual he puzzled over Joe neglecting to keep a score.

Button still struggled even though he knew the effort to be useless. He dived and rolled and all the while the Messerschmitt remained on his tail. Bullets had already thudded into the armour plating behind Button, and now the German closed again. Button rolled the Hurricane once more; this time the enemy bullets caught the tip of his starboard wing and Button could see the streams of fabric steadily lengthening in the wind. He looked in his mirror: the Messerschmitt had banked to keep with him and appeared to be closing again. Button no longer felt frightened; the imminence of death had jostled his fear away. He prepared to take avoiding action again yet his mind was clear enough to wonder what he was trying to avoid — not death, since this had become more real than life.

Button's eyes remained on the reflection of his executioner in the mirror. And suddenly he saw smoke gushing from the Messerschmitt and in the same instant another aircraft flashed through Button's mirror picture — a Hurricane. Button banked; the Messerschmitt was already falling, flames now flooding its fuselage, and away to port the Hurricane was turning into the attack again. The enemy fighter tumbled towards the mountain, exploding amongst the scrubby pines, and Joe dropped to join Button, waggling his wings. Button felt no gratitude for his deliverance; instead terror came tearing into him again.

Perowne left on a second mission immediately his aircraft had been refuelled. This time he flew with only Shaw and Lawson, leaving Osborne to curse the malfunctioning engine of his Hurricane. Perowne returned thirty minutes later, four minutes before the other two members of his section, the edges of his wings smeared with gun soot and his ammunition expended in a strafing attack on the Monastir-Salonika road. Three Hurricanes were taking off as he landed — Joe, Jimmy and George — and he learnt that the squadron was already on the move to a new field, even further south near Amfilokhia. Retreat was accelerating.

Simon provided him with the latest news. 'The Greeks in the Salonika area seem virtually finished. They've been blasted to hell. Wilson is moving in his left flank, pulling back on Kozani and Gravena, and he's sending the New Zealand Division further south to hold the passes north of Mount Olympus. I tell you Teddy — it's going to be Larissa next.'

121

Perowne hauled himself back into his Hurricane. Button, Shaw, Lawson and Osborne moved into line behind him, with Osborne insisting that his engine had been patched sufficiently for the flight to the new airfield. To Perowne's left, Simon was climbing into the Anson; tents had already been pulled down. A Greek farmer stood by the stone building which had served as the Operations Room, presumably waiting for the pilots to depart so that he could claim possession for his goats again.

ELEVEN

Osborne disappeared on the flight south to the new airfield at Amfilokhia. Nobody saw him go or heard a last message over the R/T: he'd simply been swallowed in the mist still cloaking the mountains. The squadron had seven pilots left, and the machines which they had to fly were becoming increasingly unreliable: Perowne's engine faltered during the flight, and Lawson complained that his Hurricane lacked full power.

Now the smeared and stained Hurricanes were scattered along the perimeter of the latest airfield and Perowne and his pilots stood in a small group surveying the miserable scene around them. Amfilokhia seemed even more unsuitable that the previous squadron camps. The olive groves which surrounded the area provided some cover for the aircraft, yet at the same time restricted landing and take-off space. Perowne had found that he'd been obliged to come in sharply, and the moment his wheels touched the olives loomed ahead, so that he had to start braking immediately, jerking up the handle then releasing it quickly when the aircraft threatened to nose over. Trenches were dug in the trees, spreading out into the open, and Greek women from the nearby village were still spading out the dark brown earth. They worked in silence, hardly glancing at the newcomers, and most of them wore black. Perowne thought that from a distance they seemed like crows, pecking the soil for worms.

The pilots walked to the edge of the field and sat on the rocky ground beneath the trees. They ate a meal of tomatoes and minced goat meat, washing the tough chunks down with retsina. The German aircraft came when Perowne had just put down his tin plate.

They heard the faint drone of Dorniers and then the unmistakable moaning whine of Messerschmitts. The distant dots appeared through the broad pass to the south; already the pilots were on their feet and running through the olives, zigzagging between the gnarled trunks to reach their machines. Joe's Hurricane moved out into the open followed by Shaw and Lawson almost together. Joe roared down the field and began to lift; Shaw, Lawson and George left as a trio close behind. Perowne waited a moment for Jimmy Riley and Button to move alongside him, and the first bombs were already blasting the olives to the south as these last Hurricanes prepared to leave the ground.

Two bombs exploded beside the airfield as Perowne's wheels left the earth. He banked sharply above the green stunted branches and glimpsed more bombs erupting in rapid succession along the field. He could hear Joe on the R/T. 'Messerschmitts to port, coming in fast. Climb with me George.' Shaw spoke to Lawson: 'Come on Louse, let's bugger the bastards. Take the left and I'll take the other ...' Perowne moved his own R/T to transmit. 'Jimmy, Button, stick with me. We'll go for the bombers.'

One Dornier had completed a run above them and was banking gently to starboard. Another roared over the field at the same height as Perowne, its bombs exploding amongst the trenches. A third followed, dropping steadily towards the end of the field, and Perowne twisted towards it: the Dornier and the three Hurricanes approached each other on an almost direct course. Perowne caught the enemy in his sight, and as he did so noted a black shape moving up into the corner of his vision: he glanced quickly to port and saw Jimmy's Hurricane alongside him. Jimmy's guns fired; Perowne knew the range still to be too great. Jimmy fired again, and this time Perowne joined with him. Their streams of tracer flicked towards the bomber, catching the starboard wing and central

124

fuselage, and immediately the enemy's nose tilted forward. Perowne pulled back his stick and rose above the doomed Dornier, noticing as he did so that Jimmy had rolled to follow the bomber down. The enemy aircraft hit the ground, flinging burning wreckage amongst the trenches: Jimmy climbed to join Perowne and as the second Hurricane came alongside Perowne could see the boy's excited wave; he lifted his hand from the stick in brief reply.

The sky had suddenly cleared. Perowne looked above to port and starboard and could only locate two Hurricanes flying a mile or so away off his port beam. He looked below: the Greek women were already running from the trees to fill in the craters blasted in the landing path, with the black figures streaming from all sides of the field to converge on the ugly eruptions. Perowne and Jimmy continued to circle while the tiny workers toiled below; the two pilots were joined by Button, suddenly appearing from the south, and then by Joe and George. At last Simon's voice reached Perowne over the radio: 'OK Teddy, you can try a landing. But it's still a hell of a mess down here.'

Perowne led the way. His wheels skimmed the first crater and touched just before the next to bounce over the rough soil and to touch again beyond; he braked, the aircraft tilted as one wheel sank into soft earth, and he straightened the machine, braking again to steer between a cluster of freshly-filled craters towards the trees. Perowne opened the cockpit and remained in his seat, watching his pilots drop down one by one.

Joe landed precisely into the open space and barely needed to correct his run; George came in with equal precision; Jimmy bounced badly but managed to retain control. Then Button approached. He made one low run over the field and began to drop from the trees, only to pull up at the last moment to start another attempt; this time his wheels touched and snagged, and the Hurricane

125

slewed sideways to port yet somehow remained on its wheels. It began slithering to starboard with Button still trying to brake; the machine bounced, the tail-plane lifting then crashing back to the ground, and the lamed aircraft continued to slide. Another crater lay in its path, fresh soil spilling from the brim; Perowne watched helpless as the wheels of Button's Hurricane rolled over the edge, and the nose dropped abruptly with the propellor grinding viciously into the earth. Mechanics were running forward, and Perowne glimpsed Simon limping amongst them. Three Greek women reached the aircraft first, gathering their skirts in their hands as they struggled to climb onto the tilted wing.

Perowne, now sprinting with the rest towards the Hurricane, saw Button slumped forward in his harness. Someone smashed open the canopy. Perowne caught the sickly stench of the over-heated engine and he shouted at the women to clear out of the way since the Hurricane might explode. Simon was already pulling one woman from the wing. But another had reached inside the cockpit to help drag Button from his seat and out into the open and down to the ground. Button sagged into her arms, his legs struggling to give him support; the old woman and the boy shuffled slowly away.

The Hurricane failed to erupt. It remained lodged at its crazy angle, intact but useless, and in the silence which followed the landings Perowne could hear the steady tick of cooling metal. Shaw and Lawson returned ten minutes later after having chased the enemy through the mountains to the north, bringing down a final Messerschmitt — their fourth in the engagement — with their remaining bullets. They bumped safely into land still flying together.

Button's arm was badly broken just below the elbow. He sat propped against a trunk by the side of the field, and Perowne squatted beside him. The youngster was being nursed by the old woman, his skin seeming white and clean in comparison to her walnut face as she bent over him. Gently she bound his arm tight across his chest, her eyes showing pity as he groaned with the pain.

'At least you're out of it Button,' said Perowne. 'No more flying for you for a while.' The boy made no reply and continued to bite into his lower lip with the pain. The old woman helped him hold a mug of tea, then she stood to join those who were already levelling the craters in the field.

By now the cost of the raid had been counted. Wreckage from the Dornier smouldered in the trees along the eastern edge of the field, and amongst the glowing embers lay the remains of five or perhaps six Greek women. Machine gun victims were crumpled in the trenches like piles of old rags, the black dresses soaked even darker by blood. Others were grouped beneath the olives, their wounds being bandaged, their lined and wizened faces startling white. They refused help from Perowne and his pilots, saying nothing but simply waving the men away when they approached. One or two of the survivors wailed softly in anguish until shushed by their companions; Perowne walked back to Button, leaving the women still poking and raking amongst the Dornier ashes for the shreds of bodies.

Other Greek women were still working in the open when the Messerschmitts roared from above the olives, unseen and unheard until the last shattering moment. Four fighters thundered into view, flying line abreast, bullets raking the earth in parallel tracks. Some of the women began to run for cover, hampered by their long skirts; others crouched to the ground; others simply stood. The clatter of the attacking aircraft reached a crescendo, then faded but only to be replaced by the rising noise of engines as they approached again.

Perowne, squatting beside Button, saw an old woman half-running towards the false shelter of the tilted Hurricane in the crater. She slithered beneath the angled fuselage; Button scrambled to his feet and attempted to run forward. Perowne flung out his arms to grab the boy's legs, bringing him to the ground, and at that moment the fighters swept above them with bullets shredding the dusty olive leaves and spitting onwards, over the women in the field, the noise drowning any screams. The Messerschmitts banked and disappeared; moans and whimpers and the crackling of flames replaced the howl of their engines.

Perowne stood to look at the carnage before him. Then he glanced down. Button lay beside him, two holes punched into his naked back, his neck gashed open with the white of bones visible amongst the glistening red, his skull battered in; flies were already beginning to settle.

Nine women had died from the machine gun fire. Others were terribly wounded, and three couldn't hope to survive the night. Included in the worst wounded was the old woman who had sheltered under the Hurricane; the aircraft remained intact. This time the pilots helped the women to lay the bodies on the eastern edge of the field, and amongst them they placed Button and three dead mechanics. Perowne and his men sat and ate their tasteless food, their faces still coated with dust and grime, and then they lay down to sleep beneath the trees. Night fell with the living stretched on one side of the airfield, the dead on the other, and with the constant sound of gunfire mingling with the crackle of dying flames and the clicking of the cicadas.

Simon woke Perowne an hour before dawn. Light from his torch glowed on his facial wounds, making the healed skin seem raw again. 'I've managed to contact GHQ' he said. 'It looks bloody awful.' Perowne sat up, the map between his knees, using the thin beam from the shaded torch to pick out names as Simon spoke. 'It seems that the 12th and 20th Greek Divisions have had it in the Salonika area. They've held out as long as they can, but it's no go. The Jerries are pressing hard and there's a great gap between the Greeks and the British. Wilson is having to fight unsupported. He's pulling back, right down to Thermopylae. But it's a hell of an operation. The troops have to make it through Larissa to reach Thermopylae and the bottle-neck there could be a death-trap. It all depends on the rearguard holding the Germans before Larissa, and that means here, in the Mount Olympus area. The New Zealanders are to hold the passes. And we've got to give them all the bloody help we can. At least you have. Christ – I wish you'd let me fly.'

Perowne folded the map. 'We haven't even an aircraft for you.'

'Give one of the youngsters a rest.'

'There's only one of them left – Jimmy – and he's doing pretty well. We need you on the ground.' Perowne struggled to his feet, his legs stiff and cold through the night in the open. 'Come on Si,' he said. 'Help me sort out the sections.'

The squadron flew from the airfield in a continuous succession of missions northwards over the mountains. Another battered Hurricane squadron joined them during the first day after their arrival at Amfilokhia, and next morning the pilots joined in a single section after an appeal for help arrived whilst insufficient aircraft were on the ground. The missions continued throughout that day and the next, one sortie after another in a bewildering procession; four times during this period the airfield suffered strafing attacks, and the other squadron lost two aircraft destroyed on the ground plus two which crashed when pilots were bringing them in to land during a sudden raid.

Perowne and his pilots found it impossible to assess the military situation, except that affairs continued to slide rapidly in favour of the enemy. Before, it had been reasonably easy to discover troop movements and dispositions; now, no one seemed to know. The pilots merely flew to designated points on the map and came back without any real knowledge of where they had been. Appeals for help were continuous, and could never all be met, nor could one be distinguished from another.

Perowne's pilots remained six in number. Shaw received an ugly leg wound but insisted he could still fly. 'While the Louse is up there, then so am I.' Perowne didn't argue: Shaw and Lawson gave each other strength. Perowne himself was almost too exhausted to judge the condition of his men and instead relied on Simon, who watched them fly away and waited for their return. Simon noted the way in which Joe attempted to smile at Lawson's rough jokes, the way in which Jimmy tried to copy Joe's behaviour and mannerisms, including the habit of smoothing his long hair back from his forehead, and he also observed George's withdrawal further into himself.

'George always was a funny sort of bloke,' said Simon to Perowne. The two men were squatting beneath the olives; dusk had dropped over the airfield, quietening at last the constant roar of aircraft, and the black mountains seemed to be pressing in beyond the trees. Simon sucked his pipe. 'Both George and Joe are too damned quiet, but with Joe it's a matey sort of quiet. George gives me the creeps sometimes. And he's getting worse — never says a thing all evening. Just broods.'

Perowne smiled. 'We can't all natter as much as you. And George is damned tired.'

'No more than the others. I tell you he needs watching.'

Fighting intensified north of Larissa as the British

rearguard attempted to block the German advance. Another squadron arrived at the Amfilokhia airfield early one morning, amounting to just four machines which had survived a massive Luftwaffe assault on the main airfield near Larissa the previous day, 15 April. Each time Perowne's pilots flew north, they could see the steady stream of British army traffic on the roads towards Thermopylae. It seemed the Larissa bottleneck had been safely passed by the main units, but appeals for help from the rearguard still sent the pilots deep into the forbidding ranges of Mount Olympus. Bad weather allowed some respite for two days, but then the Germans pushed with renewed vigour. Confusion increased; gradually the rearguard began to fall back.

Darkness had dropped on another frenzied day. Perowne found George sitting with his back against an olive tree, his hands on his bent knees, his face pale as he bent back his head to receive the breeze. He'd said nothing since his last R/T message during his final mission, an hour ago. Perowne sat beside him; both remained silent until Perowne suddenly said: 'We seem to be making out. No pilots or aircraft lost for four days. We might survive after all.'

'We'll not survive.' George's voice was matter-of-fact.

'Don't be so damned gloomy. Things will buck up.'

'You know they won't.'

'Things have been bad before – remember last year.'

'This is different.' George was silent again for a moment; then he began to speak, his voice still emotionless. 'We haven't a chance. Everything is against us. Everything is on the side of the Huns – even the Gods.'

'The Gods?'

Teddy could sense the smile in George's voice. 'Yes – haven't you noticed? This is where they live – always was and always will be – and they're watching us. And they don't like us.'

'You must be joking.'

'Perhaps. But I'm surprised you don't feel something. I do. They watch us and decide which of us will be next. They play with us, and we can't do a damn thing about it.'

Soon after dawn next day Joe flew with Jimmy Riley beyond Larissa. Ahead lifted the foothills of Mount Olympus, still dark around the first slopes, pink light catching the higher ground. Joe led the way up through the rising valleys; below the roads appeared almost deserted, but in the hills Australian and New Zealand troops still struggled in the narrow passes as they attempted to extricate their rearguard. Joe's Hurricane veered west, clearing the first ridges and seeking the Tempe gorge where the 5th New Zealand Brigade was calling for help. To the east soared the peak of Olympus itself, with the summit capped by cloud, and Joe remembered George's words late the previous night: 'You come closest to the Gods on Olympus. It seems sacrilegious to fight a battle there.'

Jimmy suddenly shouted over the R/T. 'Bandits! Bandits above! Two-three Messerschmitts.' Joe located the enemy immediately: the Messerschmitts were flying about 5,000 feet higher than the two Hurricanes, apparently oblivious to their presence. 'We'll leave them be,' said Joe. 'Three against two isn't good odds and we're needed elsewhere.'

'For Christ's sake – they haven't seen us.'

'Then we'll go before they do.'

'Like hell we will. I'm going up.' Jimmy's Hurricane suddenly boosted into a steep climb; Joe was obliged to follow, and the two aircraft angled upwards with the rising sun behind them. Joe allowed Jimmy to lead the way. The three enemy aircraft were flying in loose formation heading west and with one slightly behind the others. The Hurricanes approached rapidly at full power, climbing over 2,000 feet each minute and closing into the enemy's blind spot beneath and to the rear of the cockpit.

'Jimmy. You take the back marker. I'll go for the other two.'

'OK. I'll help you when I've dealt with the last bastard.'

Jimmy's exhilaration had increased during the climb. He felt as if he were leading a section into combat, and even though the section only comprised one other aircraft, that aircraft belonged to Joe. Joe had hesitated to fight; Jimmy whispered to himself 'he must be getting jittery'. His own confidence had increased accordingly, and now the Messerschmitt swung into his sights with the enemy pilot ignorant of his approach. Jimmy had somehow misjudged his angle of climb, coming up too far behind the enemy machine, but he felt he still had the advantage; he levelled and began to close on the Messerschmitt's rear. Jimmy prepared to fire, calculating exactly the best moment: too soon, and he might miss. The enemy aircraft grew in his sights. His thumb stiffened; he fired.

And in the fraction of a second before that instant, the German pilot had flipped to port in a beautifully executed evasive action, and Jimmy knew that his approach had been observed from the very beginning. The German had even increased his speed slightly during Jimmy's approach, to bring his opponent further to his rear and therefore into better view through his mirror. And the enemy pilot had timed his evasive movement perfectly: if the Messerschmitt had moved too soon, or too late, he would have been shot from the sky. As it was, he'd gained the advantage, and for the first time Jimmy felt a tremor of fear: his opponent was a better pilot.

Already, Jimmy was banking hard, trying to turn as tight as possible so that he could face his enemy.

He searched about him in near panic, glimpsing Joe's Hurricane away to port with the other two Messerschmitts, and then he located his enemy. The Messerschmitt was on Jimmy's beam about half a mile away, closing fast, and would be opening fire within two seconds. Jimmy, in those slithers of a second, knew that if he either dived or attempted to climb he would be overtaken and destroyed. He had a last moment of courage. He kicked his left foot on the rudder bar, hauled the stick back and hard over to the left, and the Hurricane twisted directly towards the Messerschmitt.

The two aircraft approached at a closing speed of over 500 miles per hour. The first to pull away would be dead, exposed to the full fire of the other. And in that fleeting, infinitesimal passage of time Jimmy experienced total terror; he whimpered once, like a puppy; sweat dribbled from his chin. Then, almost involuntarily, Jimmy's hands moved the stick, suddenly jerking the column back and into his stomach, and the nose of the Hurricane rose to block the sight of the enemy. The Messerschmitt's bullets blasted into the Hurricane's naked belly. Jimmy felt the balls of fire carving into his legs and thighs and his world exploded.

Joe's victim floated downwards, the parachute drifting gently away from the mountain with the white face of the enemy pilot clearly visible as the Hurricane circled once around him. The wreckage of the Messerschmitt had dropped deep into a shadowy cleft on the hillside. Joe's other opponent had already disappeared; he searched for Jimmy, having seen nothing of his death. Two miles away, over the slope of the mountain, the ruins of an aircraft were burning, and Joe flew low in a vain attempt to identify the remains − the aircraft could have been German or British. He called Jimmy on the R/T but could only hear the distant chatter of other

134

dogfights, and he headed down the valley away from Olympus.

The wreckage on the mountain still smouldered when Joe flew over again later that day. This time Perowne led the section, with George his Number Two and Joe weaving behind, and as the trio had lifted from the airfield Perowne realized that they comprised the remaining flying survivors of the Dunkirk days. Now another retreating British army struggled beneath them, and the help which Perowne and his pilots could offer remained pitifully small; the enemy seemed stronger than ever, and it seemed retreat would never end. Perowne tried to concentrate on the mission ahead, but his thoughts constantly returned to those who had flown behind him in the past, and were gone – so many names, so little achieved. Now the awesome and mysterious slopes of Olympus loomed ahead, the cloud hanging even heavier about the summit, swirling and fingering the crags as if determined to hide the secret of the mountains from mortal eyes.

George also studied the approaching mountain. Perowne's Hurricane, moving ahead and to one side of his own, appeared puny in comparison with the spectacle beyond. The Gods had chosen wisely in selecting Olympus as their home. Amongst those clouds lived Zeus, scorning the more gentle slopes of Parnassos to the south, home of Apollo, God of the Sun. With Zeus went darkness and foreboding and the threat of tempest. And to George it seemed that the Hurricanes intruded the privacy of the Gods, and the pathetic human struggle in the passes below served as an affront to the dignity of the dieties dwelling in the heights.

Joe's aircraft lurched in the turbulent air; the clouds appeared to be reaching up towards him, black at the base and with the westerly wind tossing the upper layers. He checked his altimeter – 15,000 feet: soon

Perowne would begin his descent through the clouds to the battered 5th New Zealand Brigade rearguard. Joe took another look around his cockpit, as he'd done so many times before, checking the gauges, switching on his reflector sight, registering almost automatically that everything was normal.

'OK Orange Section. Here we go.'

To Joe, Perowne's quiet words seemed an echo of Dunkirk, of the battle for France, the final evacuation from Cherbourg, the dogfights over southern England, the battles with the bombers reaching for London, the missions over the Channel. . . .

The three Hurricanes broke through the cloud at 3,000 feet. Perhaps they came down too far to the north and therefore over the German positions, or perhaps the battle line had shifted southwards without Perowne's knowledge, or perhaps New Zealand gunners believed these aircraft to be German – Perowne and his pilots would never know which of these three alternatives was correct. But as they dropped beneath the cloud they saw the masses of anti-aircraft fire flashing on the ground below, and around them burst a carpet of orange explosions and evil black blobs; it made no difference whether the guns below were New Zealand or German. Perowne attempted to dive deeper, with Joe and George peeling in line astern on his tail.

The gun flashes formed a bright chain in front of Joe's eyes. He believed it would be all or nothing – either he would be blown from the sky or he would survive. Neither happened. Instead his Hurricane suddenly tilted forward almost onto its back, as if a giant hand had grabbed the tail to flip the machine over, and pain careered through Joe's body with wetness flowing warm from his ribs. His eyes blurred.

'I'm hit.' He spoke the words to himself, then managed to switch the R/T knob and repeated them. He struggled to level the machine but found it difficult to

136

turn, as though the giant were still holding the Hurricane's tail. Perowne's voice cut into his dazed mind. 'How bad is it Joe?'

'Don't know. The rudder seems damaged. And I've caught something in my ribs.'

'Can you make it southwards?'

'I'll try.'

'We'll be with you.'

Joe banked to port, the Hurricane floundering as he manoeuvred, and the gun flashes diminished beneath him. He struggled to clear his mind. The pain in his body seemed centred on his left side at the base of his ribs, and he glanced down to see the jagged tear in his sweater with blood seeping over the dirty white wool. Waves of dizziness surged stronger.

'Teddy. I think I'm going to pass out.'

'Hang on Joe. Do you want to jump?'

'Not yet. We might still be over the Jerries.'

The ground swept by beneath them, rising and falling as they flew over the foothills of Olympus; Joe's Hurricane slithered to port and starboard and he guessed the tail unit must be severely damaged; gradually the aircraft sank lower and Joe's chin fell further onto his chest.

'Joe! Lift her!'

Joe shook his head again. 'I think I'll have to go down. She won't respond. She's becoming impossible to fly. I've no strength to fight her.'

By now the Hurricane flew too low for Joe to jump, even if he'd felt able to open the cockpit and climb from his seat. He glanced upwards, and saw Perowne's aircraft on his beam with George beyond.

Perowne spoke again. 'There may be a possible landing spot ahead. Look – over the next ridge.'

Joe saw the ridge and the ground falling beyond to a small valley, running in the same direction as his flight path and with the fields in this dip showing greener

137

against the yellow of the hills. Then his eyes blurred again; he gripped the stick tightly to retain contact with consciousness.

'I'll try it,' he told Perowne. 'It'll have to be first go – I can't bring her round for another bash.'

The Hurricane cleared the ridge at less than fifty feet and Joe eased forward the stick to follow the contour of the land as it fell beyond, with the field steadily filling his hazy vision. He pushed the stick still further and adjusted the throttle; his indicator showed just over 100 mph, dropping rapidly. Now he could see stones littering the sparse grass; the rough ground suddenly leapt up at him. The wheels touched and immediately the whole aircraft smashed heavily onto the earth – the tail wheel must have been shot away, thought Joe; the aircraft skidded, bounced and jolted to shoot fresh pain through his body. He jerked the brakes and the machine shuddered, bounced again; Joe pulled the brakes with all remaining strength. Thuds reverberated beneath the fuselage. At last the Hurricane came to rest.

'Joe – are you OK?'

'I think so.'

'You'd better get out. Can you manage?'

'I'll try. I'm switching off now.'

Joe unplugged the R/T lead, disengaged the harness and reached for the canopy lever. He gasped as pain screwed through his ribs; he tried again and managed to reach the catch, and he sat panting with his fingers clutching the metal, then tried to open the canopy. Twice he tried, and after the second vain attempt he slumped back in his seat with sweat drenching his face and with the cockpit spinning before his eyes. He knew he'd never be able to summon sufficient strength.

Joe lifted his head as an aircraft roared low above him and he watched Perowne banking south of the field to circle once more. Beyond, the clouds of Olympus were even darker than before, blackened by thunder and

138

by the approach of night; light rain dropped on the cockpit perspex. Joe plugged in the R/T again, to hear Perowne's anxious voice.

'. . . do it. You must keep on trying Joe. Joe?'

'I'm here. I can't manage it.'

'Try again.'

'It's no go. Teddy — you'd better be off.'

'I'm not leaving you.'

'Don't be so crazy.' The effort to talk was bringing dizziness again. 'I'm switching off Teddy. Cheerio. See you sometime soon. Take care.' Joe used his remaining strength to unplug the R/T and silence swamped the cockpit, broken only by the faint patter of rain on the canopy and the moan of the mountain wind. At last Joe allowed his head to slump and the waves to wash over him.

Joe never heard the machine nor the sound of someone clambering onto the Hurricane's wing. The swaying of the aircraft as it took the man's weight seemed merely to be the rocking of the wind. Joe only raised his head when metal smashed harsh against the canopy and the cover began to grind back, pulled by the man whose shape appeared black against the murky twilight, and then Joe fumbled for his revolver gasping again with pain.

'Joe — can you help?'

'Teddy! What the hell are you doing?'

'What does it look like. Give us a hand.'

Between them they managed to slide back the hood. Drizzle dampened Joe's flushed face. Teddy reached inside; Joe clenched his teeth as the other pilot pulled him gradually from the cockpit and out onto the wing. Teddy helped him to the ground and half-carried him beneath the shelter of the aircraft to lay him on the stony ground. Both men looked at the damaged tail-plane: the rear half of the unit had been torn away on a level with the rudder controls and now hung useless.

Perowne bent to uncover the wound in Joe's side. 'Leave it Teddy,' said Joe, 'at least for the moment. Let me get my breath back.' He lay quietly, his rapid breathing gradually subsiding, then he said: 'You shouldn't be here.'

'I know.'

'I would've been OK.'

'Like hell you would. The Germans will soon be here. I couldn't leave you sitting like a pregnant duck.'

'You should be back at the airfield.'

'I've told you – I know. You sound like George. Had a hell of an argument with him. He said the Gods would look after you – something crazy like that. I said I'd rather have a bash myself. My Hurricane's over there, right as rain. George will tell them you've had a prang, and we'll have you away in the Anson.'

'Not tonight.' The darkness had thickened so that Joe could scarcely see Perowne's face.

'Perhaps not. Tomorrow then.'

'If the Germans don't come first.'

George headed directly towards the home of the Gods. In front rose the black clouds of Olympus, boiling into the darkening sky. He began to ease back the stick to climb above the storm, and it was then that his engine started to falter: first he thought he'd imagined the Hurricane's missing beat, but the stutter sounded again, growing more staccato as he continued his attempt to climb. He pushed forward the control column again: something must be wrong with the carburettor float, he thought, and he forced his mind to act in its normal rational fashion. First he checked his position on the map, then he examined the sky around him: to port the clouds were massed as thick and as black as those in front; the sky appeared lighter to starboard and this direction would therefore be the best to take if his faulty engine prevented him from rising above the foul

140

weather. But this route was also the longest. George checked his fuel level: if his malfunctioning engine proved greedy he would have no chance of reaching the nearest airfield. George looked in front again. He'd made his decision. He would invade the home of the Gods. And behind his logical calculations, his rational choice, lay another motive: George wanted to tempt the Gods. Always, they had the power to select him as the next to die; now he wanted to pre-empt their selection by offering himself. George's physical and mental exhaustion seemed to drop away as he headed towards the thunderstorm.

Within four minutes the turbulence caused the Hurricane to drop a dozen feet or more, with the wings creaking as they struck the base of the pocket. George struggled to keep the aircraft level, but the nose bucked once, then higher. By now the clouds were swirling thick around him and rain drummed on the canopy. He felt the aircraft slipping sideways, to the east, and he remembered that the Ancients had a name for this prevailing westerly wind blowing from the mountains — zephyrus, bringer of life. Now it threatened to bring his death, forcing his faltering aircraft to the peaks below.

The white clouds were streaked with black, like marble. The aircraft plunged into these ugly fissures and they turned into bottomless black pits; George pulled at the stick, the engine missed again, and the Hurricane lurched with even greater violence. Blackness enveloped the pilot and his frail machine, deeper than night, and the rain lashing against the cockpit swelled into the roar of a waterfall in spate. The thunder of the torrent merged with the thunder of the clashing black clouds, crashing into George's ears; he had no idea of direction or height, no sensation of moving forwards, only of sinking and being thrown upwards again by the bubbling air below.

Vivid streaks of flame seared his eyes as the lightning

suddenly flashed around him, reflecting on the sodden wings and on George's hand as he gripped the stick. He knew himself to be in the grasp of the Gods. Outside moved Zeus, mightiest of all Gods, who threw thunderbolts at those who dared to confront him – Zeus, who overthrew the thirteen Titans in the assault on Olympus and cast them into Tararus, the most horrendous pit of Hades. And now Zeus clutched the pathetic midge-like machine which fluttered in the midst of his clouds, and his fingers closed to crush the troublesome mite.

Yet Zeus wearied of his anger. The aircraft was unworthy of his wrath, too insignificant to warrant his attention. He therefore flicked it aside. The Hurricane fell from the fingers of Zeus, broken and lifeless, spiralling from the thunderclouds into the twilight, with the pilot twirling inside the cockpit desperately attempting to level his dead machine. Two thousand feet above the earth George abandoned the struggle. He slid back the hood, threw apart his harness, and plummeted into space to drop like Icarus with melted wings until the parachute suddenly halted his headlong fall. George drifted down with the west wind taking him gently away from the mountain and into the softer darkness of night.

TWELVE

Gradually the black clouds rolled away leaving the summit of Olympus silhouetted against the starlit sky, and the rumble of artillery replaced the thunder of the storm. Streaks of white and yellow light flashed to the north, but now this lightning issued from approaching German guns. The two pilots still sheltered beneath the Hurricane's wing.

Perowne turned Joe on his side and gently pulled away the sweater and bloodstained shirt to expose the shrapnel wound. The wet red gash seemed to shimmer in the moonlight against the whiteness of the surrounding skin. Perowne's fingers touched the opening and pressed lightly, and Joe clenched his hands in the effort not to wince.

'There doesn't seem to be anything in it. It's deep, but clean. And I can't find any broken bones. You were lucky – an inch or so towards the centre and it would've made a terrible mess.'

Perowne tore the remains of Joe's shirt into rough strips and fastened the ends together to make a long bandage, then he folded a handkerchief to act as a pad against the wound. He helped Joe to sit upright, and the boy rested his hands on Perowne's shoulders whilst the other encircled his slender waist with the improvised dressing. Perowne drew the cloth as tight as he could, tying the ends around Joe's stomach. 'That'll have to do,' he said, pulling the sweater down over Joe's head again.

Joe had begun to shiver as the night air struck his skin. He lay back still trembling, teeth chattering as he tried to talk. Perowne found the boy's cigarettes and lit one for him, drawing deeply himself before passing it over. 'Don't try to natter,' he said. Then Perowne took off his own sweater and spread it over Joe, despite the other's protests. He lay close beside him, and the warmth from each of their bodies joined to give them greater comfort, and they waited for dawn with the night sky a huge dome above them.

Anna adjusted the blackout curtain covering the studio window then switched on the lamp. The glow from the light reflected warm on Susie's skin. The girl sat enveloped by a blanket, hair flowing onto her half-covered shoulders, legs bent beneath her on the rug-covered mattress.

'Are you ready?' asked Anna.

'I suppose so. I still feel very shy.'

'You needn't be.'

'I only thought you'd want to sketch my face again.'

Anna smiled. 'Not when the rest of you looks so good.' She placed the pad on the easel and sharpened the charcoal stick before walking forward to bend over Susie. Gently she took hold of the blanket and lifted it away from the girl's naked body. Susie's hands dropped to her sides. Anna held the girl's shoulders, turning her slightly, then stood back to look before bending again to alter the positioning of the knees. She could feel the soft warmth of Susie's skin as her fingers brushed against her thigh.

Anna's charcoal moved rapidly over the pad outlining the girl's body. She tried to capture the sweep of her hair and the matching slope of her shoulders, and the curve of her breasts. The charcoal moved to the slender waist and to the swell of the hips and down to the strong lines of Susie's thighs with the darkness between. Anna provided the face with more detail – the large, slightly oval eyes, the tilted nose, the wide mouth with lips just parted in an expression of almost surprise. Anna wanted to depict the innocent promise which the young body offered, the desire to give combined with uncertainty over the emotions and perhaps pain which this giving entailed, a

144

woman's instinctive passion mingled with a young girl's inexperience. Anna wanted to reveal the reason why men should desire the girl in front of her.

And as Anna worked, her eyes moving from the paper to Susie's body, she put herself in the position of a man, and she began to react accordingly. She herself felt the desire which Susie provoked. She imagined Joe's reaction to the naked girl, and in her concentration this imagination became reality. Her hand hesitated over the pad and the charcoal strokes became less confident, until Anna placed the stick on the easel ledge and stood wiping her dusty fingers on her skirt.

Susie smiled. 'Isn't it going well? I told you I wouldn't be a good model.'

'You're fine. It's me.' Anna added: 'I'll try again in a moment – you can move if you like.'

Susie stretched, her elbows bent and her back arched, no longer shy. Anna walked slowly across the studio and sat beside her on the mattress. 'I could never sketch you as I'd like. I see you there, but I can't get it down.' She turned to look at Susie. Gently she reached forward and traced her finger down the curve of Susie's neck, leaving a faint trace of charcoal dust. She took her hand away for a moment to wet her fingers on her lips before returning them to Susie's skin to clean away the smear, and this time her touch continued lightly over the swell of Susie's breast.

Susie sat motionless, watching Anna's face. She could see the desire in the other girl's eyes and could feel the tremble in her fingers. She felt no distaste at Anna's actions, no revulsion, instead bewilderment. Then Anna's fingers moved lower to follow the curve of the breast and Susie could feel her skin tightening in response, and her body which had desired Joe for so long began to welcome a touch which could have been his. She closed her eyes and her breasts rose and fell, then her thighs slipped apart, and Anna leant forward to gently awake, the

145

passions which were impatient for life. The rug felt soft as Susie settled slowly back. Her eyes were still closed, her legs were stretched wide, her hands lay by her sides. She still felt no sense of shame, instead wonder at the awakening of her body as Anna moved softly over her with fingers and lips. Anna said: 'Don't open your eyes,' and Susie felt her hand being lifted. Her fingers were closed round the other girl's breast; she looked up to see Anna kneeling naked beside her, and still with wonderment she began to touch Anna as she herself was being caressed.

So the two girls lay and loved, marvelling in the beauty of the other which each knew they also possessed themselves, conscious of the pleasure which they gave and received, thankful for the respite in their loneliness. Susie came to know something of the excitement which she would share with Joe; Anna's senses woke for a moment from the sleep caused by Teddy's absence.

Anna stood and turned out the lights, then pulled away the blackout curtain with her body outlined against the window. She returned to Susie, and they pulled up the rug to hold one another and to lay looking at the sweeping night sky.

Dawn began to lighten the summit of Olympus. Perowne was already awake. He looked down at Joe beside him, noting the pallor in the boy's face. Gunfire still thudded from the north and had become noticeably louder; twice during the night Perowne had seen flashes to the south followed by the echo of artillery, which could only mean that at least one German unit had pushed beyond Olympus towards Larissa. Outlying patrols might already be probing towards them. Perowne pulled his map from his flying-suit pocket and tried to guess their position, peering at the paper in the half-light: he found a valley which appeared to be the one in which they'd landed, then he frowned with anxiety when he

146

noticed a track running less than two miles to the west – the route curved round Olympus to join the Larissa road, and might easily be used by the Germans.

Light swept stronger down the mountain. And now Perowne heard the crackle of small-arms fire somewhere to the west. Joe stirred at the sound and attempted to sit.

'What's that?' he asked. 'Sounded like rifles.'

'I think it was.'

'You'd better be going Teddy.'

Perowne made no reply. The crackle came again and he attempted to estimate distance and direction: he reckoned the firing must be about two miles over the ridge, somewhere near the track. He looked down at Joe. 'How does your side feel?'

'Better. Doesn't hurt as much when I move – you made a good job of it. And my head's clear.'

Perowne checked the bandage: blood had seeped through one edge, drying stiff, but the bleeding had stopped.

'Teddy – leave me now.'

'I'll wait a while longer. Someone should soon be here with the Anson – George must have got back before dark last night.'

Joe lay back again, realizing it would do no good to argue; he dreaded the loneliness which would sweep over him when Perowne's Hurricane dwindled to the south. His eyes wandered along the length of the battered aircraft fuselage above him to the ruins of the tail-plane and to the shattered section still hanging by a thread, swaying gently in the morning breeze.

Staccato shots echoed in the hills. A long, raking burst of machine gun fire followed almost immediately, finally drowned by the hollow crump of mortar bombs exploding beyond the ridge, and Joe believed he could hear the faint murmur of vehicles.

'Teddy – for Christ's sake don't leave it any longer.'

'They must be pushing along the track. Perhaps they'll

147

stick to it.' Perowne showed Joe the map and their position. Joe lay back again and said: 'The shots seemed closer than the road. There's some kind of opposition – they'll try to outflank, and it'll bring them this way. Go on Teddy, I'll be OK.'

Perowne looked down again at the pale face of the boy beside him. He felt tempted to offer his own aircraft, but knew it would be refused. He glanced at the sky, searching for signs of the Anson but seeing nothing.

'Go on Teddy. The Anson is bound to be here soon. There's no point in you staying.'

'I'll give it five minutes.'

The minutes stretched to ten. Three more mortar bombs thumped over the ridge together with the more brittle explosion of grenades. The machine gun chattered at frequent intervals; once Perowne thought he could hear a whistle being blown. And then silence fell, gradually broken by the rising sound of a vehicle moving in high gear. Once Perowne walked to his machine and tried to contact RAF units over the R/T, but interference proved too great, as it had done with previous attempts made by Perowne during the night. Perowne walked slowly back to Joe's crippled machine. Still no Anson appeared over the southern horizon.

'OK Teddy – that's it. Get the hell out of it.'

Perowne rose to his feet, then bent to adjust Joe's bandages again. He crouched for a moment beside the other pilot; Joe grinned up at him.

'I'll see you later Teddy.'

Perowne merely nodded as he stood to go. A vivid memory flashed across his mind – of Henny crumpling forward in his cockpit when the advancing German infantrymen opened fire in the French field. Perowne turned once more and unbuckled his revolver, tossing the weapon beside Joe; then he walked quickly away.

Joe watched the Hurricane taxiing into a take-off position. The engine reached a deeper roar as Perowne opened the throttle, and the aircraft jerked forward to bounce over the stones and into the air; Joe twisted his head and continued to watch as Perowne banked swiftly to starboard and disappeared over the ridge. Less than a minute later Joe heard the Hurricane's machine guns, one angry burst after another, and then the aircraft rose into his sight again two miles or more away and gradually the speck faded into the haze. Joe lay back. The sun had risen further over the mountains, and now the light angled around the edge of the fuselage above the pilot to fall warm on his face. Joe reached out to the revolver which Perowne had left, placing it next to his own, and he settled to wait.

Perowne began his airfield approach and as he neared the open space between the olives he saw fresh damage from Luftwaffe attacks. Women moved aside from his path when he levelled between the raw craters; his Hurricane lurched on impact and his tired arms fought to control the machine with the olives beyond the airfield rushing to meet him. He braked once more and half-slewed the machine to a stop, and he cut the engine.

Simon was limping forward as fast as he could when Perowne slid back the canopy.

'For pity's sake – where have you been? And where's Joe?'

'Isn't George here?'

Simon shook his head. 'We thought all of you must have bought it. It's bloody good to see you – but where's Joe?'

Perowne hauled himself from the cockpit, telling Simon the news. He dropped from the wing to the ground and took out the map to show Joe's position; already mechanics were attending to his Hurricane.

'So I need the Anson quick,' continued Perowne. 'There's still a chance I can pull Joe out. But the Jerries were swarming down that track. I used all my ammunition on them, but it wouldn't stop them for long.'

'The Anson's gone.' Simon pointed to the wreckage in the trees. 'It bought it early this morning. The bastards have been over twice already.'

'Then we must get another two-seater.'

'Where the hell from? There's no aircraft left. There's a hell of a flap on. The Greeks have surrendered.'

News had arrived just before dawn of the capitulation: all major Greek units had disintegrated under the German pressure, many groups fighting to the last man. Now the full weight of the German advance would be thrown on the British at Thermopylae.

'Shaw and Lawson are already over there,' continued Simon. 'Orders are for all available fighters to give maximum support. You'd better be on your way Teddy. There's one spare machine – take that while your's is being tarted up again.'

'I can't leave Joe.'

'You can't do anything for him. He's had it Teddy.' Simon turned abruptly and began to limp back towards the shelter of the battered trees.

Joe still lay beneath his Hurricane. He could hear vehicles again, and now the distant whine of tanks; firing had finished; the German advance would push rapidly forward once more and soon the enemy must reach the ridge above the valley, and the Hurricane would be plainly visible.

The pilot's eyes remained on the stained fuselage of the aircraft above his head. A fly buzzed in his ear, and he brushed it impatiently away, wincing again from the ache in his side. The heavy section of shattered tail-plane now hung motionless; Joe examined the damage almost with disinterest, until suddenly his eyes narrowed in concentration. He pushed himself into a sitting position and began to crawl towards the rear of the aircraft; still on his knees he reached up to the trailing section and tested its weight, and the feel of the metal in his hands confirmed his guess. This dragging, useless encumbrance had been mainly responsible for the Hurricane's erratic behaviour, making it almost impossible to fly the machine. Once removed, the aircraft might be operable but only on a relatively straight line – and only if it could be made to drag itself forward into the take-off lacking the rear wheel.

Joe helped himself up by clutching the flank of the fuselage, and he hurried towards the front of the aircraft. He managed to climb on the wing and to reach inside, fumbling for the few tools stowed in the pocket beside the seat. He clutched them to his chest and carried them back to the tail, and he began to unscrew and wrench apart the hanging section.

The squealing, whining Panzers were now clearly audible, together with shrill whistles as infantry officers signalled their men. Joe kept his eyes fixed on the work in front of him; twice he had to stop and rest, wiping the sweat from his face with his grimy hands, and all the time he expected fire to burst from the hillside behind him. The useless metal refused to become completely detached. Joe's side throbbed with increasing violence and he could feel the wetness on his hip as the blood flowed again; he forced himself to be calm and not to attack the damaged section in futile panic.

A whistle sounded so loud that Joe involuntarily wrenched round his head. The slope remained empty and he turned to his task again, still without success. He felt tempted to run and try to hide, but the barren valley offered no cover. The spanner slipped in his sweating hands.

One part of the section suddenly swung free. Joe tugged the remainder, without result. A thin shout reached him; he glanced over his shoulder but no-one could yet be seen – the German infantry must be climbing steadily on the far side of the gentle ridge and must be within yards of the easy summit. Pain punched through Joe's body as he wrenched vainly with the spanner again, and he sagged to his knees, his strength gone, his head reeling, lacking even sufficient life to unbuckle his revolver.

An RAF corporal ran from the olive trees with two messages for Perowne as he prepared to leave on his mission over Thermopylae. George had just telephoned from a village near Elasson into which he'd hobbled with a broken ankle just before dawn: he would be hitching a lift south with the New Zealand rearguard. Perowne passed the second message to Simon, standing beside him: the signal fluttered in the warm wind as Simon read the words.

'GHQ BEF TO ALL UNITS. TIMED 900 22/9/41. EVACUATION FROM GREECE BEGINS 1700 HRS TODAY. PRELIMINARY WARNING. DETAILED ORDERS FOLLOW. ALL RAF OPERATIONS CEASE NOON. ENDS'

Perowne glanced at his watch. Within two hours the RAF struggle would cease; already the effort was ineffectual with only a handful of machines and men against overwhelming Luftwaffe supremacy. Perowne began to climb into his cockpit, for perhaps the last time in Greece. The battle was almost over and was long since lost. Shaw and Lawson were fighting over Thermopylae, but whatever they did would be useless, and he himself must join the futile attempt. Perowne, Shaw and Lawson were the only remaining operational pilots in the squadron. Joe must now be dead or captured. The squadron was finished. Perowne closed the canopy above him and the engine of the Hurricane burst into life.

Simon watched Perowne's machine slip out of sight beyond the trees; he stood alone at the edge of the airfield, and his thoughts remained on Joe, alone amongst the enemy. Soon the few survivors in the squadron, pilots and ground crews, would be leaving; Joe would remain, his body rotting on the slopes of Olympus.

The Greek women were continuing their efforts to keep the airfield intact — efforts which were now wasted since the Germans would soon be in possession. A solitary Hurricane stood as a reminder of the squadron's presence. Simon's eyes remained on the machine, the aircraft in which Perowne had returned that morning and which had been readied for continued fighting. It would no longer be used.

Simon suddenly began to walk, dragging his leg across the churned ground. He shouted at a mechanic to fetch a helmet; two more were told to prepare the Hurricane for immediate take-off, and they ran to position the chocks in front of the wheels. Simon was helped onto the wing and he shook his head impatiently when someone attempted to hand him a parachute; he eased himself into the cockpit, smelling again the scent of war which he'd once known so well; the engine clattered and thundered into life, and Simon signalled at the waiting airmen holding the chock ropes as he boosted the revs. The unleashed Hurricane pounced forward.

Joe sensed rather than saw the presence of the Germans behind him. He jerked his head round: the first infantrymen were outlined on the summit of the ridge, five hundred yards away, a section of eight or more in an irregular line. They seemed to be hesitating, uncertain whether the lone Hurricane in the valley might be part of an ambush. Joe continued to sag on his knees, clutching his wound, the twisted tail-plane section hanging in front of his face.

Someone shouted and another voice answered. Slowly Joe shuffled round to face the enemy again. More men had joined the others on the ridge, extending the line, and Joe could see two soldiers crouching, perhaps beside a

153

machine gun or a mortar. Still no shots shattered the silence of the valley, and Joe guessed that other Germans were working their way round on either side of him: the single Hurricane must seem a too obvious target – the Germans still feared a trap and were guarding themselves with typical efficiency.

Perhaps five minutes dragged by although the passing of time seemed infinite. Then, with appalling suddenness, the machine gun started its cacophony and bullets whipped the ground on the far side of the Hurricane. The sound was multiplied by the echo from the hills. Joe slid to the earth, wincing as he pressed against his wound. The burst ended in abrupt silence; Joe presumed the German soldier would be correcting his aim and preparing to squeeze the trigger again.

A fraction of a second existed between the invisible roar of the Hurricane and the sudden shape of the aircraft as it climbed the slope and flashed into view. Its Brownings blazed from its angled wings. It began a tight turn almost as soon as it came into sight, diving a second time on the exposed German infantrymen. The Hurricane's assault jolted Joe into action: he found himself on his knees attacking the metal again, the scrape of his spanner mingling with the clatter of the Hurricane's guns behind him. Now Joe worked in a frenzy, wrenching and tugging, forgetting the stabbing pain from his wound. Bullets flayed the soil beside him but he scarcely noticed.

The metal fell free, thudding to the ground. Joe dropped his spanner and struggled to his feet, clutching his side. He ran the length of the fuselage and crawled on the wing to fling himself into the cockpit. His hands grabbed for the controls; he closed his eyes as if in prayer as he sought to start the engine. The Hurricane vibrated beneath him and suddenly became a living animal eager to leap into the air, and both pilot and aircraft ignored their wounds as they struggled in a final bid for survival.

Joe boosted the throttle and began to move, trying to turn the maimed aircraft into the wind; he glanced out of his cockpit to see the second Hurricane diving once more to his right. German infantrymen were hurrying down the slope towards him, some of them stopping to kneel and fire before running again.

At last Joe had positioned the aircraft for take-off. He kept the brake tight, boosted the throttle to the maximum possible, then suddenly released the brake lever. The Hurricane lurched forward, dragging its wheelless tail, tilting first one way then another as it snagged against stones; Joe adjusted the propellor at full fine and set the carburettor boost for maximum power, and all the while the machine swerved and swayed, crashing repeatedly against the ground until it seemed the whole structure must split apart. Joe's reactions were immediate as he fought to retain control. Speed gradually increased, using the benefit of the valley slope. The wheels left the ground, smashed down again, then the earth dropped away and the wind rushed with increasing violence past the open cockpit. Fabric on the port wing suddenly fluttered and began to stream as machine gun bullets mashed through the metal, and below him Joe glimpsed the white faces of German infantrymen as they raised their rifles, but he swept onwards to freedom.

Joe headed down the valley. His aircraft remained unwieldy, slithering about the sky in a drunken fashion, and sweat saturated Joe's clothing as he grappled with the controls. He felt his arms becoming weaker, and his senses began to fade, and the agony of his wound caused his breathing to break into short panting gasps. The horizon lifted in front of him as the nose of his Hurricane dropped steadily towards the fields.

'For Christ's sake Joe. You fly that thing like a one-armed monkey. Can't you manage any better than that?'

'Simon! God it's good to hear you!'

'Well then, don't make it all a waste of time by pranging that thing. Keep her nose up. Try a bit harder damn you.'

Joe forced his words through his semi-consciousness. 'We'll swop if you like.'

'I'll leave her to you. You'll make it with a bit of advice. Come on – keep talking.'

So the two Hurricanes flew south-west away from Olympus, over the plain of Thessaly, over the Pindhus peaks and the lonely Akheloos river twisting in its narrow valley between the mountains, and they began to drop towards the green of the western coastal strip and the airfield of Amfilokhia. Simon forced Joe to keep talking and to retain consciousness. Only once did Simon's voice lose its bantering tone, and by then the olive groves of Amfilokhia had slipped into sight.

'You're nearly there Joe. I think only you could've done it. I knew you would.'

'Now he tells me.'

Long before the airfield Joe had begun to manoeuvre his crippled machine into the correct landing course, and slowly the Hurricane slithered into the desired direction. Joe knew he would only have one landing chance: with half his tail-plane missing he could never circle for another approach. Now the Hurricane dropped steadily, still slewing one way then the other. The final olives almost brushed the battered undercarriage and seconds later the aircraft pounded the ground with a massive grinding crash. Joe could feel the machine sliding away from him, the controls virtually powerless in his hands. He jerked the brake, once, twice, then again; the aircraft skidded broadside and further into an almost complete circle, beginning to slide backwards on its mutilated tail. Suddenly the remains of the slithering tail ploughed into soft soil, filling a bomb crater, and the superstructure dug into the ground. The aircraft stopped abruptly then cracked apart somewhere to the rear of the fuselage and

156

buckled together like a concertina, at last becoming motionless.

Joe slumped over the column, his gasps punctured by retching. Hands reached inside the open cockpit and dragged him out, and only then did Joe feel his trousers flapping wet against his thigh, sodden by blood from his re-opened wound. He stood for a moment looking for Simon, and saw him sagging exhausted against his own machine. Joe walked slowly across, and the mechanics let him go alone; the two pilots walked away from their aircraft each supporting the other.

Perowne started out from the trees to meet them. He stopped, watching them limp towards him, knowing they preferred to come without help. Joe's waxen face, almost yellow with weariness, made him look younger than ever; despite his own exhaustion Simon's mutilated body seemed to gain strength from the boy's need of him. Perowne glanced around the airfield, now almost deserted. Shaw and Lawson had already gone, heading for Athens and for evacuation to Cairo; George would soon arrive and then they too would leave for North Africa. Shaw, Lawson, George, Simon, Joe and Perowne himself – all that remained of the squadron, and of these men only three were physically fit to fly. Perowne walked the few paces forward to Simon and Joe, thinking again that the squadron had surely been destroyed. It had always been obliged to fight in retreat or on the defensive – Dunkirk, France, southern England, Greece. It had never been allowed to taste victory, and now it seemed it never would.

THIRTEEN

Perowne walked across the compound at GHQ RAF Middle East. The Cairo air struck warm and moist, sticking his shirt to his back. Smart uniformed RAF personnel hustled through the corridors as he opened the swing doors to the main administration block; fans whirred overhead. The place reminded Perowne of a hospital, and he felt clumsy and alien. His awkwardness increased as he waited to be shown into the office of Air Commodore Matheson, Senior Staff Officer to the Air Officer Administration.

Matheson rose to shake hands when Perowne entered his spacious, sparsely furnished room.

'Good of you to come so soon.' He motioned Perowne to a chair. 'We have to decide what to do with you and your men. You've taken a hammering Squadron-Leader.' Perowne could think of no response. Matheson settled back in his chair. 'We have to make one of two choices. We can merge the remains of your squadron with another – your pilots could easily be fitted in elsewhere and you yourself are overdue for promotion. I've received word there's a Wing Command for you back in England.'

Matheson was silent for a moment, staring absently through the window at the compound beyond. 'Or we can re-build. The trouble with that is the shortage of equipment and men. As you know, this chap Rommel is creating hell up in the desert, taking advantage of the withdrawal of our forces for Greece. And the troops from Greece have been packed onto Crete, which will probably be blasted at any moment. We've hardly enough aircraft for existing operational squadrons, never mind re-building those which have been battered as much as yours.'

The Air Commodore seemed to be thinking aloud. 'On the other hand, we have to be optimistic. Did you hear the Prime Minister's broadcast last night? Marvellous. Talked about the Greek evacuation and said things would get better sometime. Finished with quoting a poem. In other words we've got to be ready to take the offensive, and that means being ready for rapid expansion of our forces.'

He turned to Perowne. 'So there we are. What do you think? As far as you personally are concerned, the first alternative will mean a step up to Wing Commander, and back home. If we re-build your squadron we'll have to keep you as a squadron leader to help sort things out.'

'I'd prefer the second.'

'So I thought. And that's the decision we've taken. Your squadron is to be operational again, Perowne – all the bumf is in this envelope.' He slipped a file over the desk.

Perowne smiled and the Air Commodore grinned in return, his face suddenly shedding the official, impersonal attitude. 'Mind you,' he said, 'there's some compensation for your postponement to a Wing Command. You can leave someone in charge here while you go back to England for a time – to organize the newcomers.'

Anna's image flashed through Perowne's mind, chased away by another vision – of a boy lying wounded and alone beneath his mutilated Hurricane. He said: 'I'd rather see to things at this end. I've got someone else who'd be better in England. Caton. Flying-Officer Joe Caton. The best pilot we've had.'

Perowne walked back across the compound, thoughts jumbling in his mind – of the squadron and its rebirth from the ashes of defeat, of Anna and her love, of George and Simon, of Susie's face when Joe came back to her, and of the forbidding future with the Germans pushing forward over the North African wilderness and poised to descend upon Crete. And Perowne wondered again how long it would be before the perilous night of retreat could be brought to an end.